brutal game

CARA McKENNA

First Edition

Edited by Kelli Collins

Cover design by Cara McKenna

ISBN 978-0-9980911-1-2

READER ADVISORY

This book contains consensual but intense
rape role-playing scenes that some may find upsetting.

CHAPTER ONE

FLYNN CLIMBED INTO HIS CAR just after one on Saturday night, waking the grumpy engine on the third crank. It had to be ten degrees out, and just the short walk from the bar's exit to the curb had chilled his sweat and stiffened his spent muscles. He could feel frost in his hair and an ache growling in his wrists and fingers. Still, he didn't bother with the heater—it was a quick drive.

It was snowing, barely. Sick as he was of shoveling, he almost wished for a final storm. It was late February, the charm of New England winter gone with the abandoned skeletons of Christmas trees weeks before. The streets were crusted with brown-gray ice and these flurries would do jack to cover it over. Salt and gravel crunched under his tires as he pulled onto the street, South Boston all but abandoned this time of night, save for the odd car in the distance and scattered drinkers making their way home with clumsy, nervous steps along the slick sidewalks.

Flynn was beat, literally. Not defeated, but he'd taken a couple hard shots in his final boxing match, one to the temple and one to the chin, and his neck was sore, like whiplash.

You're not twenty-five anymore, his body bitched, but he ignored it. He'd be home soon, in his warm apartment, with a warm woman curled up and waiting on his couch or in his bed. Maybe already asleep with a book on her chest. Maybe amenable to having that book plucked away, replaced by the weight of her lover lowering down, his lips on hers and sleep be damned.

Heat crept through him, not the radiator's doing. It kept the chill at bay as he slammed the car door and headed for his building, a hulking old brick behemoth.

Fight nights were Fridays and Saturdays. Laurel nearly always came to one or the other, whichever her waitressing schedule didn't clash with. Tonight she'd worked, and would've finished up around ten. She lived just a few blocks from the tourist-trap restaurant she worked at but she always came to his place on fight nights, letting herself in with her key and waiting up for him.

He tested the knob, pleased to find it locked. She'd been sloppy about that when she'd first started hanging out in his absence, and he didn't like it. Made him paranoid and protective, even if his building was pretty safe. The thought of anything bad happening to her, let alone in his place, with him not there...

He felt a flash of the heat that possessed him during a fight and pushed the worry from his mind as he opened the door.

Flynn's apartment was a studio—bedroom, living room, and galley kitchen all in one high-ceilinged square space, plus a full bath. Laurel was sprawled across his bed, a pillow on her belly and a closed book atop that, sock-clad feet flexing idly.

"Hey, you." Her smile was dozy and sweet, hair a coppery tumble he'd be more than happy to mess up if she'd let him.

"You win?"

He dropped his gym bag on the loveseat by the door. "Always."

"How many matches tonight?"

"Three."

"You must be wiped." She knew better than that, though. She knew what fight nights did to Flynn, the way the adrenaline turned to lust the second he stepped out of that basement gym. He might be exhausted, but his body didn't plan to rest until his cock got its way.

"I'm gonna shower," he said. "I'll kiss you when I stink less."

"I like your violent musk, but suit yourself." She opened her book. "How was work?"

She kept her eyes on the page. "It was work. Go get cleaned up."

"Yes, ma'am." He gathered a fresh tee and shorts and some flannel bottoms from the dresser then headed for the bathroom.

He needed this shower. He'd been up against his toughest rival in the final fight of the night. He'd won but that bastard always gave Flynn a run for his money, underlined the fact that he was thirty-three now, no longer invincible. They fought for glory and for fun, not for money, but that was no reason not to go hard each and every time. Flynn spent his days working construction, which wasn't kind to his body either, and in the past couple years he'd come to feel it. He ached in ways he hadn't before, even if his lust for the sport hadn't cooled a jot.

Something caught his eye as he set his clean clothes on the toilet tank—an old red towel slung over the shower curtain. Hunger rose inside him, exhaustion forgotten.

It was no simple towel. Sure, this was the towel Laurel used for a day or two after she dyed her hair each month, and the one they fucked on when she was on her period, but it was more than that. It was their little joke—the red cape. Laurel had teased Flynn about being a bull when it came to sex, and that towel was their inside joke. If he came home and found it hanging on the rod it was her way of taunting, *Gore me*. A red cape but also a green light, one that told Flynn when he exited the bathroom, it was on. The things he craved in the darkest, homeliest shadows of himself were his to take.

They had a safe word but hadn't used it in ages. Hadn't needed to. As Laurel had grown confident playing tourist in his fantasies, he'd come to know her limits as intimately as he did her body. He could read her muscles like a blind man read Braille, could tell when their role-playing was riding too sharp and thin a line between arousing and upsetting.

When you had needs like Flynn's and you wanted them met, intuition was essential. This shit was dangerous and this shit was precise, like whipping knives at a woman strapped to a spinning wheel, circus-style. Get it right or get it very, very wrong.

Which was sort of funny, he thought as he stripped, as his appetites were, after all, so very, very, *very* wrong.

He spotted a note stuck to the bathroom mirror, an oversized, lined Post-it bearing Laurel's tidy handwriting. He peeled it from the glass, eyes devouring each word.

I'm a groupie, she'd written. *I come to watch you fight every week, infatuated, but I'm afraid of you as well. You offer me a ride home but take me to your place first. You're sick of the teasing and you're ready to give me what I'm too scared to admit I want. Maybe I don't even want it at all. Maybe I'm in over my head. You don't care. You'll get what you want, either way.*

What Flynn needed in bed was cruelty and dominance. Not every night, not even every week, but the thing that lit him up like jumper cables was the dark stuff, the rough stuff. Ugly stuff it had taken him years to accept, and later embrace. Laurel had always been up for it, willing to go there and able to find pleasure in those dark places too, but over the past couple months she'd begun discovering her own kinks nested inside his.

In the games they played, he craved brutality, but she wanted something more—a narrative. A role beyond mere victim. Flynn was happy enough coming at her like a stranger in a dark alley, but her pleasure deepened with some extra dimension worked in. She wanted layers of emotion—lust clashing with revulsion and fear and surrender. She wanted a character to play, he supposed, and he wanted nothing more than for the thing that set his brain and body on fire to do the same for her.

He twisted the hot tap open and stepped inside the shower, stood under the steaming, scalding water and sighed. He eyed that red towel draped over the rod, growing dark and heavy from the spray. A gash at his temple opened and stung but he didn't care. Just let the heat soften his muscles, wash the blood and sweat and grime down the drain. Wash his fight persona away and make room for another beast entirely.

A man capable of things few women would welcome.

A man capable of exactly what Laurel wanted, tonight.

CHAPTER TWO

LAUREL STARED AT HER BOOK as much as she was truly reading it, listening to the hush of the water in the bathroom, and soon enough the tap of Flynn's toothbrush against the sink, the squeak of the medicine cabinet door. She tried to recall the words she'd scrawled on that paper, every detail of the fantasy she'd handed him. Had it gotten him as hot as composing it had done to her? Had he allowed himself a soap-slick stroke of his fist in the steaming shower, or was he saving every ounce of his fight-night aggression just for her?

Flynn appeared in his shorts and tee, silhouetted for a second before the bathroom went dark and the fan silent at the flip of the switch. By the light of the reading lamp his body was glorious, nearly too much, yet so essentially right. A *ridonkulous* body, to quote Laurel's roommate, Anne, the one time she'd come along to watch the underground fights. Accurate, but not erotic. *Obscene* about summed him up.

He looked at Laurel as he crossed the room, kept his eyes on her all the way to his dresser. He must have thought better of the pajama bottoms he'd taken into the bathroom; there wasn't anything threatening about a drawstring and an elastic waistband. It always helped to have a belt at the ready, and the tease of a zipper or stiff denim never went astray. He seemed to agree, pulling jeans out of a drawer.

Laurel set her book on the shelf behind the bed, sat up and stared back, hugging the pillow on her lap.

Once upon a time, when they'd been all but strangers, Flynn's body had scared her—she'd not yet known what his intentions were, what lay at the core of his heart and his kink. Physically, he'd been capable of doing for real the things he got off on role-playing, and it had taken a weighing of curiosity versus risk to go there with him. In the end her trust hadn't been misplaced, and oh, the places he'd taken her.

This body awed her, chilled her, intoxicated her. Whether he sought pleasure or pain, he gave himself completely. As someone who so often held herself back, Laurel found it mesmerizing.

She wondered if the game had begun. If so, it was time to quit objectifying and get into character. This wasn't her lover of eight months. This was a near stranger who both intrigued and frightened her, dangerous as a wild animal. Beautiful and bloodthirsty and hungry for who knew what. She let the scene settle in around her, tightening her belly with anticipation and fear.

She wasn't his girlfriend tonight. She was his prey.

He pulled on his jeans, still staring at her. Still staring as he threaded his belt through the loops and buckled it.

"You like my place?" he finally asked, and shut the drawer.

She looked around the room, letting its stark simplicity strike her all over again, just as it had back in July. *I've never been here before. I don't know this man beyond the bully he embodies in the ring.*

"It's nice," she said.

"How about my bed? You like that too?"

Her lips twitched and she glanced at the rumpled navy covers. "It's big," she managed, making her voice tiny, as weak as this man was strong.

"How long you been hopin' to get invited home with me?"

She swallowed. "I was just happy for the ride. I should be getting back soon."

"What's the rush?" He came closer, and she drank in how huge he felt in dark moments like this. Tall, powerful. Threatening. "You want a drink?"

"No, thanks. It's really late."

"Stay, then. I'll take you home in the morning." He sat on the edge of the mattress, and she caught a spark strike in those hazel-blue eyes when she scooted a little farther away—he was a wolf, and she the deer who'd just twitched. He craved a chase. She craved the weight of this beast crashing down on her when he got his way.

"I can't," she said. "Thank you, really, but I should get home. I could call a cab—"

"Why would you do that?" He came closer and his hand closed around her wrist, not tight, but rigid as steel—the cuff of a man who scoffed at bondage props.

"You don't have to drive me if you don't want," she said, channeling a woman too timid to call a man on his shit—the woman she'd been eight months ago, likely. It could be scary sometimes, the way the chemical rush of this role-playing so closely resembled true fear. Scary and exhilarating, and strangely freeing.

"I wouldn't offer to drive you if I didn't want to."

"It's late," she said again, letting those words fall flat and tinny with false worry.

His eyes narrowed. "You've watched me fight the past, what? Three weeks, four?"

"Not just you. I watch all the matches."

"I'm not blind, sweetheart. I see how you look at me."

She conjured the smile of a woman more anxious than amused. "You're one of the best."

"One of?"

She swallowed again. "You're the best, as far as I can tell."

"That excite you?"

"It… I don't know. Look, I think you're an amazing fighter. I'm a little drunk. I probably have some kind of crush on you, but I'm not looking to act on it. Thanks for the ride, but I need to get home."

"I asked if you wanted to see my place. You said you did. I think we both knew what that really meant."

She made to leave the bed but that hand around her wrist bit down hard, feeling like the steel it stood in for.

He said, "Don't." The word gave her chills, because she knew it'd be her uttering it soon enough. "I don't bite."

You do. "I need to go."

"A few more minutes won't hurt. Just a kiss, then we'll go. Promise."

"It's really late—" She was cut off by her own gasp, her surprise real as his hand twisted, wrenching her arm with a twinge. It lit something up inside her, a cocktail of fear and anger and frustration, and she wrestled her wrist free and made it to her feet. He liked a struggle. She'd give him one.

"I scare you?" he asked, tone eerie and casual, as chilling as if there were a jeer coloring that question.

She held her tweaked wrist. "A little."

"You came after me, you know. Maybe you like the way I scare you."

She didn't reply, letting her gaze move meaningfully to the door.

"You like watchin' me fight?" he demanded.

She met his stare. "Yes."

"What else do you wanna watch me do?"

13

She held her tongue and let that dirty, twisted hybrid of fear and excitement work through her body and settle across her features. She watched his expression darken and heat in response.

"You like watchin' me fight," he repeated, stepping close, forcing her backward until her calves found the mattress, then her ass. "What else do you wanna watch? You wanna watch me fuck?"

"I'm sorry, I didn't—"

"You like watchin' me bleed," he said, speaking low, intimate, more threat than flirtation, now. "You wanna watch me come, girl?"

Her only reply was a gasp as that powerful hand grabbed her again, clamping tight to her forearm. "Stand up."

She didn't have much choice; he all but yanked her to her feet. He was six-three and change and she was nine inches shorter, and in moments like this he seemed to loom a mile above her, godlike and terrifying.

Not a god. A monster.

"Kiss me." He said it quietly, not tenderly.

She whispered, "Okay."

His free arm circled her shoulder and he wound her long hair around his fist. Laurel shivered. That sensation did something to her, something not every rough act did. Some submissive women loved getting spanked, or held down, or blindfolded. Whatever the fuck it said about her, Laurel liked getting her hair pulled. Just feeling his hand tighten had her wishing for the pressure, the promise of domination.

He forced her chin up with a sharp yank, stared hard into her eyes with his cold ones before bringing his mouth down to hers.

It was less a kiss than an assault, but there was heat in it, too, her excitement spurred not by the smooth execution of the act but from knowing what was coming, what this promised. And knowing that Flynn was burning up inside his skin, out-of-his-mind aroused, and all because of her. The gifts she gave him weren't wrapped in satin.

They were harsh and strange and not for the faint of heart. But what they did to him made her feel as powerful as the woman she played felt helpless.

She pushed at his chest with her forearms, tried to wrest her mouth away, only to feel the bite of his fist in her hair. When he spoke, his lips moved against her cheek, breath hot.

"Don't make it hard, sweetheart."

"I want to go."

"You'll go just as soon as I've given you what we both know you came here for."

"I don't want that. I don't. Please, let me go home."

"You're a good girl, aren't you?" He eased her away from him, hand still in her hair, then forced her to sit on the bed. "One of those girls that feels too guilty to admit what they want."

"No—"

"So they find men like me, men who don't fuck around. Men who can tell exactly what it is they're really after." His hands went to his waist, freeing his belt buckle, then the button of his jeans. She made a break for it but he was on her in a blink, pinning her to the bed by her biceps.

"Make it easy, sweetheart. Your daddy or your priest or whoever you're so scared of disappointing, they're not here. Just you and me. Let yourself go."

"I want to go *home.*" It was a plea, a prayer, a toothless wisp of a wish.

"You will. Just as soon as we both get what we need. You can't tell me you don't want this. Like I don't see the way you look at me every goddamn week." He shoved one knee between hers, then the other, and Laurel felt it—her body was priming, pussy slick and ready, hungry.

"I never meant to lead you on. I never said—"

"Fuck what you said." He gave her a single shake, thumping her head and shoulders against the covers. He lowered his chest to hers. "I know what you want. You watch me fight." He breathed the words right into her ear, every syllable damp and hot and explicit. "You watch my body and you wanna know what else I'm capable of." He grabbed her hand, forced it low, pried her fingers apart and cupped her palm to his straining cock. "You want this, don't you? The one part of me those greedy eyes don't get to see."

"Stop. Please. *Please.*" Her voice was small, frail, quavering, her words like matches flicked into a puddle of gasoline—one, two, three.

"I know you," he sneered. "I know your type. You want a bad man like me, but you're too scared to admit it. You want me to give you what you need?" He stroked her hand up and down his length, so hard the friction burned. "Play your little game, make it like I'm forcin' you so you can pretend you don't want it?"

"I don't want it. I don't. Please. I'm sorry."

He put his free hand to her throat, pressing his thumb to the hollow just under her jaw. "Take me out."

"I want to go—"

"Take me out," he barked, pressing harder. "Maybe I'll let you go, if you do. But find out what you're missing first."

He released her hand and she fumbled with his fly. The zipper stuck as she pulled it down.

"C'mon."

"I'm trying." She got the zipper open and he shoved his jeans to the tops of his thighs.

"Touch me."

She was dying to but held back, waiting until a rough hand grabbed hers and clasped it to his erection. He seemed to sear her through the cotton, filling her palm, making her clench and heat, sex aching.

"Stroke it."

She did, luxuriating even as her fist moved in staggered, frightened fits and starts. He never felt half as big as he did in moments like this, flesh like iron, like a weapon. His body seemed to mirror hers; she felt the damp patch each time her palm met his head and her mouth tingled, hungry for this. Hungry for an order she prayed she'd hear before long.

His hand grew impatient, forcing her motions rougher, faster. Laurel replied only in breaths—the reedy rush of air through her nostrils, lips pursed tight.

"This what you been needing?" he hissed.

"Please. I want to go."

"Did you know I'd be this fuckin' big, sweetheart? Is this how you imagined it?"

"Please. *Please.*"

"Get your clothes off."

She froze. His hand released hers but she didn't move, lost in the role.

"Strip. Now."

"I—"

"Strip."

Again, she tried to escape. Tried to slip from under the prison of his legs and arms, but she got nowhere. A rough, broad palm covered her throat. He'd never choke her—he didn't fuck around with that shit, as he put it—but she knew to pretend he was. She went limp beneath him, eyes wide with terror.

"Strip. Don't make me say it again."

He released her neck and she reached down, wriggled her bottoms away as Flynn began tugging at her shirt. He peeled it over her arms and head, ignored her bra. He pulled his own shirt off next, and spoke to her as the cotton fell to the floor. "I'm gonna stand up, and you're not gonna move a muscle. You understand?"

She nodded, unblinking. She watched that body with awe as he ditched his jeans and shorts, standing before her in the low light, cock long and thick and ready, gleaming at the crown.

"Good," he said, cold eyes approving of her body or her obedience. "You let me and I'll make this good for you. Fight me and you've only got yourself to blame."

She held her tongue.

He clasped himself at the root. "This what you pictured, all those nights you came to watch me? You go home after and fuck yourself, hopin' I was even half this big?"

"Please."

He got back onto the bed, forcing her legs wide. "That's good. I like you better cooperative."

"You don't have to do this."

"No, I don't have to do jack-shit, apart from exactly whatever the fuck I want. This is my house. What I want, I get. You fuckin' knew that when you stepped through the door, didn't you?" His fist was stroking, hips edging their centers closer, closer. Finally, contact—the bump of his smooth head against her clit. She bucked, letting the pleasure masquerade as revulsion.

He traced her lips, no friction. "Fuck, yeah. I knew you wanted this, you lying little bitch."

She flinched at the word, a chill snaking through her. "D-don't. Please, don't."

"You feel that?" He began to push, his cock a relentless intrusion, spreading her open.

Her eyes shut and her nails bit into his shoulders.

"Yeah." He pushed deeper, deeper, in harsh thrusts until their hips met. "Don't tell me you don't want this. I feel how fuckin' wet you are."

"I don't. Please, don't do this."

He gave her his length, slow and mean. "I know you never had a cock half this big, bitch, have you? Tell me."

"Stop, pl—"

"TELL ME," he bellowed, as loud as he dared without risking a neighbor pounding on the wall or calling the cops.

"Never," she stammered. "I've never had anyone…" She trailed off.

"Had anyone what?"

"Big as you." Her voice was a trembling little mouse-squeak of a thing.

"Yeah, that's right." He owned her in rough strokes, making every inch a punishment. "Take that cock. Just like you been wanting."

She shut her eyes, turned her face away.

"Watch me fuck. *Watch me.*"

She opened her eyes to slits.

"Yeah, look at me." He made his motions long and filthy, hypnotizing. "Look at me, bitch."

All at once, Laurel craved her name like water in the desert. She often hit this wall when they indulged his kink, the work of arousal and impatience, not discomfort. She didn't want to be some stranger, some anonymous "sweetheart," some "bitch". She wanted her own name in that gruff accent, wanted it to slip free as control eluded him, same as she wanted to see helplessness glazing those eyes.

She could end the charade now, murmur "Flynn" in a telltale voice and turn this from fantasy to plain old fucking in a breath. But no. It was magic—ugly, dark, scary magic—the way this game affected him. She may be playing a powerless woman, but what she could give this man… She could turn him inside-out with a few whispered pleas. He might be on top, but she held his pleasure in her hands, as truly as she could feel his flesh under her fingernails.

His body punished hers, voice lost to grunts and moans. Her breaths had no choice but to sync with his as each thrust huffed the air from her lungs. She was dying to touch herself, praying for a shift in the angle that might rub him against her, give her relief, when—

"Turn over." He didn't give her a chance to obey. The second his weight lifted, he had her by the shoulder and arm, forcing her onto her hands and knees.

Touch me. For the love of God, touch me.

"Fuck, yeah." He held her hips and drove deep, savored for the barest moment before the brutality resumed. "You get exactly what you were after, bitch?"

"Please." Barely a whisper now.

"You feel good, girl. Don't tell me you don't love it."

She did love it, in a way. If she thought too hard about it all, things grew murky. She got caught on questions, like, what did it mean that this was the thing that turned him on like nothing else?

It means jack, she could imagine him saying. *It means the random thing my sexuality got snagged on is creepy as shit. Period.*

It didn't mean he wanted to hurt a woman, not any more than a woman who enjoyed such games really wanted to be forced. It was the taboo, the wrongness of wanting it that made it hot. Or for Laurel, it was Flynn. It was the balance of a man strong enough to hurt her for real also being the one she trusted above all others. And it was having the power to grant his darkest, dirtiest wishes, and to see and hear and feel what it did to him.

Behind her, the beast was loose and wild. His palms were slick on her hips, his cock hard in that way that only this game could make it. She longed to see his face, but more than that, she longed for selfish things. And finally, he gave her what she wanted.

He pulled out and his hands were urging her forward. "Up, on your knees. Hold the shelf." When she hesitated he barked, *"Now."*

She knew what he was after. It was something they often did when they weren't role-playing. She cast him a faux-fearful glance over her shoulder then moved, kneeling upright at the head of the bed, holding on to the edge of a shelf. He entered her roughly with a grunt that made her legs tremble. Her hair was twisted up and pushed to one side, his mouth claiming the bared side of her throat.

And finally, it came—his touch. One hand slipped around to palm her breast, the other moving between her legs, finding her clit.

"Yeah." He said it so softly, it wasn't part of the game. There was wonder in his voice, the tone that overtook him sometimes when he found her wet, or found her clit as stiff as it was now. It excited her nearly as much as the rough fingertips circling her and the thick cock gliding in and out, in and out.

For Laurel, the narrative fell away. He could imagine whatever sinful things he liked, but she didn't need anything more than exactly what this was—a powerful man using her and serving her at once. No lover had ever understood her body the way this one did. His fingers knew the exact speed, the precise pressure, his touch masterful even as his body pounded into hers, harsh and frantic. Always contradictions, with Flynn. Selfish and catering. Cruelty underpinned by blind trust. A no-nonsense, frequently tactless man, but under the surface possessing so much tenderness and loyalty and intuition.

She was losing it, falling to pieces. Her hands shook on the shelf, sweaty and crampy and weak from the pleasure coursing through her body. Her legs were water, sex molten. Her breathing came in long, low groans, sounding pained and crazed and intoxicated. She hoped maybe it was standing in for some facsimile of fear for Flynn, but honestly, she was beyond caring. All she wanted was more, more of this, until she broke apart completely.

His mouth was at her neck, just behind her ear, his breath as hot as steam. "You love that cock, girl?"

She could only gasp and pant.

"I think you do. I think you're gonna come on that cock, aren't you?"

"Please." Her last stab at feigned resistance, though that plea was genuine. *Make me come. Please, please, please.*

"I know what you need," he told her. "I'm gonna make you come harder than any man ever has."

She was dying to say his name. It echoed in her head, through her body, pulsing in every cell. It was that syllable as much as his rushing cock or taunting fingertips that pushed her over the edge.

She came hard, knuckles chalk-white where she clung to the shelf, body bucking into his, seeking and trying to escape his touch at the same time, all of it too much, never enough. Her cry was deep and animal, telling him every filthy thing she had no words for.

Behind her, that perennial chant: "Yeah, yeah, yeah," punctuating every twitch, every spasm, until she was nothing but a sweaty, trembling mess.

From Flynn, a massive groan, then, "On your back."

She obeyed, flopping gracelessly across the bed, feet on the pillow. She welcomed the heat and weight and desperation of him. Their game felt done and she held him, tugged at those same arms she'd pretended to push away not long ago.

"Fuck, honey."

She smiled to herself, slid her palms low and rode the motions of his hammering hips. "You look so fucking good."

He smiled, the gesture all but lost to the agony of his pleasure. "You're one to talk."

"You gonna come for me?"

"So goddamn hard."

"Show me, then."

She let her hands and gaze wander his body, stroking his back and arms, feasting on the spectacle of his surging cock.

"Yeah, watch me." His voice gave him away, and his half-shut eyes, the pace of his thrusts.

"Come on, Flynn."

"Yeah. Say it."

"Flynn. Show me."

"You want my come?"

"Always."

"Where? Your cunt?"

She shivered at that word. "Please."

"I like that. Beg for it."

"Give it to me, please. Deep."

His back arched and his words devolved to grunts and moans and the odd, "Yeah." He was lost, helpless, and Laurel lived for these moments.

"Come on. Please."

He sounded more animal than man, riding on the brink of madness, then all at once, he froze. He rammed so deep, Laurel winced through a cramp. Every muscle in that astounding body clenched, softened, clenched again, and ultimately went still.

She wrapped her arms around him, memorized his weight, the smell of his skin. Never let this moment cease to floor and humble her. Never let this man fail to amaze, and never let her fail to excite him. Never let familiarity curdle to boredom, she prayed.

Let this feel so easy and so wrong and so right, always.

CHAPTER THREE

FLYNN ROLLED OVER, drunker than drunk. Drunker than he'd been for real in the better half of a decade. "Fuck, honey."

Laurel chuckled and he could see the round shape of her cheek where the lamplight hit it. It made him smile in return.

"Can I ask you something?"

"You," he proclaimed grandly, "can ask me any goddamn thing you want, as long as it doesn't require me to leave this bed."

She turned to face him, rubbing his chin with her thumb and seeming to address the spot. "I feel like more and more, when we're doing the kinky stuff, by the time it's over, we're not acting."

He frowned. "What do you mean?"

"Just that by the end, we're you and me again. I'm not fighting you anymore."

"Oh. Yeah, I guess that's probably true." His chest unknotted. He'd worried she'd meant it had gotten too real for her comfort.

"Do you mind that?" she asked. "I can't figure out if I'm the one who changes things. By the time I'm about to come it's hard to pretend not to like it, is all."

"Nah, I don't mind."

"You sure?"

He nodded, then caught her lingering thumb between his teeth, biting softly.

"If it seems like I'm just getting lazy," she said, "tell me. I'll step it up."

He let her thumb go. "By the time the role-playing falls apart, I'm already as hot as I'm gonna get. The first half, that's what matters. The stuff before the actual sex, and the start of the sex. By the time it's all underway, I'm happy just bein' bossy."

"You sure?"

"How many times you gonna ask me that?"

She shrugged, studying his mouth. "I just want to make sure I'm not dropping the ball. Your kink's important to me."

"I know it is. And you don't have anything to worry about. Plus you know me—if there's something I need, I'll ask for it."

"True." She paused, then smiled.

"What?"

"You know how I can tell you're not pretending anymore?" she asked. "During the sex?"

"How?"

"You call me 'honey', instead of 'sweetheart'."

His brows rose. "Do I?"

"Yup."

"Huh." He supposed that was true.

"You used to call me 'sub shop girl'," she added.

"I did."

"And 'kiddo'. Actually, you still call me that."

"I call every woman who's younger than me 'kiddo'. But 'honey'—that's all you."

She didn't have a pet name for him, he realized. If she called him anything, it was Flynn, or occasionally Michael, but only when she was panting and overwrought, on the cusp of a violent orgasm. She liked his given name, but he preferred his last name. He'd been called that for so many years, it felt right in a way that Michael didn't. Call him "Michael" and he couldn't help it—all he heard was his shithead father's voice, drenched in Four Roses.

His sister called him Mike, which he put up with, having no choice. Looking back, it was her boyfriend, Robbie, who'd taken to calling him Flynn. He'd hero-worshipped the guy, and it was Robbie who'd gotten him into boxing, so no surprise that was the name that made him feel the most empowered, the most worthy of respect. He could've so easily been Mike or Mikey, some anonymous hoodlum selling stolen stereos out of the back of a van. Crazy what magic a strong male role model could work for a lost and angry kid.

No matter that you could probably shout the name Flynn into a megaphone from a St. Paddy's float in South Boston and have twenty people turn their heads. Far as he was concerned, that name was his. Robbie had given it to him. Given him so much and never took…not until he'd taken his own life, and far too young.

He rolled over to face Laurel, admiring the creamy glow of her bare skin, that pretty, flushed face with its sweet and wasted expression. "Christ, I fuckin' love you."

She laughed and gave his sweaty hair a limp, lazy pat. "You always say that right after we have the most depraved sex."

"That's when I'm the most grateful."

He liked things rougher than most women were down with, no matter if half the world had read that *Fifty Shades* book and decided BDSM was the new black. He was no damaged billionaire and this apartment was no tricked-out playroom. Their props were duct tape and rope and the cold, hard floor under Laurel's knees, his own two hands. Gags and blindfolds were whatever shirt he might grab, and he'd bound her with an extension cord once. This was BDSM as furnished by Home Depot, and without most of the tiresome honorifics and other formalities he found so cheesy. He didn't mind "Sir," but if any woman ever called him "Master" he'd be improvising himself a gag real quick.

He didn't want to be a woman's master; he wanted to be her assailant.

During sex, he felt all the things the sick shit he played did, hearing a lover's fear in her voice, seeing it strain her face. He'd never in a million years do this to a woman who didn't want it, but it had taken ages to get good with that distinction. To believe that it was okay to want these things, when they were consensual.

Laurel was growing drowsy and he scrunched her messy hair.

"Say it back," he said.

"I love you." The final word was swallowed by a broad yawn.

He smiled. He'd waited for her to say it first, and that must've happened back around Thanksgiving. She was cautious, reserved in some ways, not the kind of girl you rushed. He was normally the same, though he'd never been with someone who felt this right, this easy. They knocked heads now and again, but by and large all was peaceful...outside of the sex, that was.

He'd been ready to tell Laurel he loved her after maybe six weeks, but he'd known better than to have risked scaring her off. Her parents had been a real shit show, same as his, and he'd come to understand that the tighter you tried to hang on to Laurel, the more she'd edge away from you. Plus her occasional depressive bouts did a number on her confidence.

She didn't love herself the way Flynn loved her, or how her friends did. Something inside her didn't trust people who cared for her deeply. It made her feel like a fraud, or undeserving. Pretty standard, as baggage went. Plus all the practice Flynn's fucked-up family had given him at standing by difficult people made loving her feel like the easiest thing in the world.

"You remember when we first said it?" he asked.

"What? 'I love you'?"

"Mm hm."

"I do indeed. It was October thirtieth."

He blinked. "That early? You been keepin' a diary I don't know about?"

"It was the day before Halloween, I'm pretty sure. We were lying right here, and I'd had, like, three beers, and I was going on and on and *on* about all the costumes I'd made myself as a kid. And I caught myself, and I caught *you*, how you were just listening, asking me questions, letting me be drunk and sentimental and boring and acting like you were actually interested."

"Maybe I was."

She laughed. "No sober person would've been. But it just hit me, out of the blue. I think there was some complete non sequitur, like, 'And when I was eleven I went as Lisa Simpson,' and then a big dumbfounded pause and, 'I love you.'"

"'I love you, *Flynn*,'" he corrected.

She smiled. "I'll take your word for it."

"Same as I'll take your word it was October. We didn't wait that long, did we?"

"No, not really. Three months?"

"You say that to many guys before me?"

"Two. How many women did you say it to?"

"Just one."

"You mean it?"

"Yeah," he said. "I did. Did you?"

"One of them, yeah, I meant it. The other one, I meant it, but I also didn't really know what I was talking about. I think I was mostly infatuated."

"Who was he? I'll kill him. Tomorrow. After breakfast."

She snorted. "Down, boy. He was my high school boyfriend. Who did you say it to? That woman who taught you all about rough sex and stuff?"

"No, not her." She'd meant a lot to Flynn, and he had loved her, had felt that, but he'd known it wasn't that serious to her. She wouldn't have said it back, and he'd spared the both of them the awkwardness of underscoring how mismatched their investments had been.

"Who?" she asked again.

"My first serious girlfriend. The one I half-traumatized, wanting to fake-rape her all the time."

"Oh, right."

"Who was the second guy you said it to?"

"Someone I dated in college."

"Why'd you break up?"

"I can't remember, exactly. I just remember he annoyed me by the end, and I think I bummed him out. The second half of college was really hard for me. I'm surprised I made it through, looking back."

"You're at least twice as strong as you give yourself credit for."

"Probably."

"You're the first woman I've said that to since I was man enough to know what the fuck it really means," he offered. And since he'd truly known who he was, and what he needed from a lover.

"Aw. Well, you're the first *man* I've said it to, period. Both the other boyfriends were, like… I dunno. Dudes."

"Tell me I'm better in bed than either of them."

"Oh my God, yes. I feel like I never even had sex before I fucked you."

"I love you."

She laughed. "It's true. I mean, not like I'd never been given an orgasm or anything, but *fuck,* Flynn."

He grinned, all lit up inside.

"It's like I thought I knew what a strawberry tasted like because I'd smelled a scratch-n-sniff sticker of one. But you…"

"Never stop talking."

"Not that fucking you isn't a little terrifying," she said, "but you've absolutely ruined me for every other man on the planet for all time."

"My work here is done."

* * *

Laurel woke with the sun, which was to say, late. The winter light looked lazy, more slinking through the blinds than shining. She wished she could stay in this bed, beside this warm man, all day. But such was not reality.

She rolled over, shoving at Flynn's arm until he did the same and let her spoon him.

His work had him up around five most mornings, and even with the punishment of fight nights he was awake by six on the weekends. "You slept in," she said through a yawn.

"Not entirely. Mostly I've just been sitting here, watching you sleep." He said it in a creepy, breathy voice, and wrestled around to take a dramatic whiff of her hair, sending her into giggles. He knew she found that trope laughably disturbing.

She poked his chest. "Gross. Why do people think that's a sexy thing for a guy to do in books and movies? Watch a woman sleep?"

"Stalkers must do well in fiction."

"Very. But believe me—I know and trust and love you, but if I ever wake up to find you sitting beside me on my bed, just staring at me…"

"Dumpsville?"

"I dunno. Just… Just be jacking it, please."

He laughed.

"Have the decency not to pretend like it's broody and romantic. Perv all-in. If not, yes, Dumpsville. Population: you."

"That go both ways?"

She considered it. "The thing about reversing the genders on pervy bullshit is that while the woman would still seem creepy as fuck to other women, the dude she was victimizing would probably be stoked, because he could get laid."

"Feminism's complicated."

"Not complicated—complex. And don't act like you're not one. You're a product of the matriarchy if I've ever seen one." He'd been raised by his charmingly domineering older sister from puberty onward. "Plus if you didn't know how to treat women with respect and consideration, you'd never get your way in bed."

"Fair."

"You, my darling, would be creepy as fuck, if not for your feminism."

He shushed her, pulled her to him for a kiss Laurel refused to part her lips for. He might not care about her morning breath, but she did. She stroked his rough jaw and cheeks, wondering as always how he'd look with a week's stubble, the beginnings of a beard. Sadly, he shaved every morning he was working.

"Hang on," she said, regretfully leaving the covers. She'd not gotten around to putting anything on and could feel goose bumps breaking out all over her body as she scrambled for her tee and pajama bottoms. "Jesus, it must be fifty degrees in here."

"Thermostat's set to sixty-two."

"That's barbaric. If I ever move in with you, I'm reprogramming it."

"Small price."

She glanced his way to catch him grinning. He'd already invited her to move in, when she'd been bitching about her landlord hiking the rent again. It was Laurel who wasn't quite ready. For one, her apartment was six minutes' walk from her job. For another, one of her two roommates was her best friend. Plus being here when Flynn wasn't... There was something lonely about it. Maybe it wouldn't feel that way if she moved her stuff in and there was a TV and she could listen to her music, but all the same, she wasn't there yet. Whether she could stand Flynn twenty-four-seven, that wasn't an issue. It was whether or not he'd be up for *her* around the clock that worried Laurel. Maybe that was insecurity talking, or maybe pragmatism. Either way, she wasn't yet ready to find out which.

She brushed her teeth and tamed her hair, bumped the thermostat up to sixty-eight before climbing back under the covers.

"Oh, so warm. Let's just hibernate until May."

"When do you need to be at work?" He kissed her neck.

"Ten."

He eyed the clock on the shelf above their heads. "Let's see... Twenty-minute shower, ten-minute drive... That leaves nearly an hour for fucking."

"Hang on, now—factor in putting on makeup, drying my hair..."

"Your hair'll dry during the fucking."

"I think I'll earn better tips if I don't look like I've got a red bird's nest on my head."

"Fine. Still leaves plenty of time if we shut up and get down to it."

"Fine." Better than fine. She'd been especially horny of late, probably her body finally getting used to the Pill, or just the benefit of being on the far swing of the depression pendulum, maximum distance from the next inevitable blue phase. Might as well make the most of the hormones while they were on her side. "Let's get filthy, then."

"Not too sore?"

She shook her head and tousled his short hair. "Nope. I feel sturdy." Physically and emotionally. She felt that way more and more, since meeting this man. Crazy how dabbling in such dark fantasies seemed to purge some unseen, unnamed weight from her subconscious. Or perhaps that was just the ease that came from feeling safe in a relationship, accepted and supported. And lusted for.

"Hang on—brush your teeth," she commanded, and gave his bare butt a good smack when he climbed over her to comply. She watched his body as he crossed the room, all that winter-pale skin and improbable muscle. Way more man than she'd ever imagined she wanted, and so much so that if this affair ended, replacing him would be no less than impossible. No chance *two* men built like that would be fool enough to fall for her in one lifetime. Her karma wasn't bad but it wasn't spotless, either.

He emerged from the bathroom in all his naked glory, eyebrow raised pointedly.

"What?"

"No note on the mirror?"

"I'm not that creative this early in the morning." Or that disinhibited without a drink or two. "Can we just do plain old fucking?"

"Always." He all but pounced on her, the covers shoved aside and hands seeking skin—hers warm, his cold. She yelped and laughed and squirmed and they kissed until the ice in his touch melted away.

"How do you want me?" he asked, a low and familiar growl in his voice.

"On top." She couldn't always get off first thing in the morning, but she'd stand the best chance if she got to watch that body working above her, that gorgeous, mean face staring her down and her right hand free to assist.

He moved his legs between hers. "You need lube?"

"Probably."

He snatched the bottle off the shelf, and if his fingers were cool, the gel was *frigid*.

"Ah, fuck."

"Don't think about it," he breathed, easing two thick fingers inside her. "Think about this."

Indeed. Or think about what those fingers promised but could never approximate. She looked between them, to the half-hard cock between his thighs. She closed her fist around him. If her hand was cold, he didn't show it. His eyes shut and his head dropped back, and his groan made her feel like the one on top, the one with all the power. He added a third finger, driving inside her to the rhythm of her strokes. In a minute flat she was all but panting for him.

"I'm ready."

"I'm not," he murmured, eyes on his hands, plundering her sex.

She squeezed his stiff length. "Liar."

"Don't rush me."

"Tick-tock, Flynn."

He knocked her hand aside with something approaching a snarl and fisted himself, angled his crown to her lips. He sank deep, not too fast, but not slow enough. A twinge tensed her and she stilled him with a squeeze of his arm.

"Slow. Just to start."

"Sure."

He was different when they weren't role-playing, but in some ways much the same. He was always intense, whether he was issuing orders or holding her down or propped above her in the sunshine, smiling. Just now he was caught somewhere between tender and impatient, his cock easing in slowly even as his eyes shone with need.

"Better?"

"Yeah. I'm good." She squirted lube onto her fingertips and he sped up. She watched his body in the silvery morning light, marveling that this room had ever seemed cold.

"Fuck, you feel good." He close his eyes, hips beginning to rush.

"Ooh." Another cramp jabbed her, the shock of it stealing her breath.

He stopped. "Too rough?"

"Too deep, I think… I'll get there. Just give me a minute."

Always the picture of control, he kept his thrusts shallow. Laurel got lost in her own pleasure, in the glorious view, in the sounds of his soft grunts and the smell of his skin and—

"Oh!" A cramp to put the first two to shame.

He slowed. "Okay?"

Her legs seized up, stilling his hips. "Hang on."

He paused, cock seated deep and pulsing sharply, like a wild creature feigning patience.

"It hurt?"

"I'm crampy. Really crampy. Ow, ow ow ow." She squeezed her eyes shut as her body twinged around him.

He eased out. "Better?"

She released a breath and nodded. "Yeah, thanks. Jeez, that was new. Felt like you were jabbing me right in the cervix."

"Sexy."

"You're huge, but still, that was weird."

"Is it because of how rough it got last night?"

"No, probably just some Pill side effect. Like maybe my period's decided to turn up after all."

His brow furrowed and he moved to sit beside her. "Turn up? You mean it's late?" That stern expression froze her solid for a beat, but wait, no. Silly. No need to panic.

"Periods don't really come late when you're on the Pill," she said. "They come or they don't. My first cycle, I skipped it entirely. Another time it only lasted a day. That's pretty common. But I do feel PMS-y." The horniness was unusual for that time of the month, but she'd also had an achy back and a general feeling of off-ness the past couple days, of spacy distraction.

"I'd have to google it," she said. "Maybe your period can come late if your body's still getting used to the hormones..." The more she spoke, the deeper the barbs of doubt pricked.

"You don't sound too sure."

"It's really, really unlikely that I could be..." She didn't even want to say the word aloud. "Though I guess I could pick up a test after work, just to put our minds at ease."

"Maybe."

Weird. She'd never taken a pregnancy test before, never had any reason to.

What if I was? she wanted to ask. *Pregnant.*

She had less than a speck of a clue what answer she'd hope to hear from him.

A baby was simply not an option at this point in her life. The only thing about it that made sense was that this man should be the father.

"It's *really* unlikely." She said it to soothe herself as much as Flynn. "I haven't missed a single pill." She kept them in her purse, paranoid about forgetting them some night when she was crashing at Flynn's. Took them each evening at the same time she flossed her teeth, using each chore as a cue to keep her from skipping the other.

"Up to you," he said.

"I'll see how I feel after work. Speaking of which, let's get you taken care of. Clock's ticking."

Though his cock was still hard, he smiled and shook his head. "Not half as fun if I can't get you off. You want my mouth?"

"No, my brain's kinda hijacked, now. Thanks, though. But seriously, we can do you. I don't mind."

"You're sleepin' over tonight, right? I'll save it up."

"Oh good, I'll be in for the mauling of a lifetime."

He grinned. "You know it."

"Right. Let me hop in the shower and we'll get this show on the road."

"You want coffee?"

"I'd *love* coffee, thank you."

Flynn didn't drink caffeine but he'd bought a coffeemaker just for her. A steaming mug was waiting when she emerged from the shower, dressed, a towel turbanned around her head. Flynn owned a hairdryer too, and she sometimes wondered who he'd bought that for originally, since he certainly didn't use it. She liked to tell herself it was for shrink-wrapping the windows come winter or some other such manly, practical purpose, but it was nearly March and the view of the neighboring brick was as crisp as always.

Whatever. Every lover he's had has made him the man he is today. I ought to be sending out thank-yous.

The man himself was nowhere in sight, which meant he was either chatting with his sister three floors down or doing something with his car. It always felt intimate and strange to be in this apartment without him. Like she was snooping, even though she never had. If she wanted to, it wouldn't take long; he was the most minimalist person she'd ever encountered. If she moved in here, her possessions would make this lofty space feel instantly cluttered. And far more like home.

She turned at the sound of the key in the lock and smiled. He'd probably been gone for all of ten minutes, but the overprotectiveness charmed her. It was a novelty to someone who'd grown up with a mother as detached and careless as Laurel's.

He was wearing a knit cap and his canvas jacket, cheeks burned pink. "Fuckin' freezing out there."

"Hard to believe it'll be spring in a few weeks. You warming the car up?"

"No, checking on Heather's." Heather was his sister. "She said it wouldn't start and it looks like she's right."

"Bummer. Hell of a week to get stuck waiting for a bus. Can you fix it?"

"Probably not, unless it just needs a jump or something. If not, I'll get it towed for her and give the mechanic the stink-eye so they don't try and overcharge her."

Laurel smiled. "There should be a name for the opposite of feminine wiles. They get the same results."

"How's the coffee?"

"Delicious."

"The key," he said, crouching to slide a massive phone book from the bottom of his bookshelf, "is to put in way more grounds than you're supposed to."

"Or stop buying Dunkin' Donuts coffee. It's so watery, no wonder you need twice as much."

He glowered, eyes on the pages he was flipping. "You take that blaspheming mouth out of New England, woman."

"I'm from Providence—I get to say it's awful."

He set the Yellow Pages on the counter. Flynn was the only person Laurel knew who actually kept a phone book in the house. It was one of the many reasons she loved him. He owned a computer but barely used it, even though she'd insisted he finally get internet so they could stream movies.

"Almost ready?" he asked, eyeing the Auto Garage listings.

"Just let me chug this and dry my hair, and I'll be good to go."

"I'll warm the car up. Meet me down there."

"Will do. Five minutes."

He left Laurel be with her coffee, and the second the door shut her head filled up with way too many questions. Was she actually queasy, or was that her imagination? Or was she just queasy with uncertainty? Either way, the coffee wouldn't help. Neither would spending her shift trying to decide whether or not to pick up a pregnancy test.

"It's really unlikely," she told the coffeemaker.

You've said that three times, the red light seemed to reply. She switched it off.

"Like, really unlikely," she said, making it four. And she'd keep on saying that until she believed it.

CHAPTER FOUR

SUNDAY WASN'T MUCH OF A DAY OF REST. Flynn dropped Laurel off at her work, back just in time to drive his sister and niece to church. By early afternoon he had Heather's car entrusted to a neighborhood garage, and after a grocery run, he headed off for his near-daily workout.

The gym was the same venue where he fought each weekend, a shady little concrete-and-cinder-block outfit in the basement of a shitty bar. On Sundays it was usually just him and the younger guys, everybody else doing the family thing.

The family thing. Sprawled on a weight bench, he stared up at the ceiling, at the bald fluorescent bulbs staring right back. Though neither of them had spoken of the question of a pregnancy test since Laurel had disappeared for her shower, he hadn't quit thinking about it for a second.

Flynn's mental baseline was a sort of anxious thrumming, not unlike the buzzing of the light above him—an ever-present hum that never let up, aside from when he was fighting or fucking. It was the reason he didn't drink coffee, which only made him more of a punchy motherfucker than he already was. Alcohol turned him into a mopey dick, and he wasn't about to go back to smoking a pack a day after kicking the habit once. He supposed a marijuana scrip wouldn't be so hard to snag, but that stinky-ass shit was for hippies and burnouts. That eliminated the most popular chemical crutches. Physical release was all he had left, and so here he was every day he wasn't in the ring, punishing his body until his brain could finally shut the fuck up.

The pregnancy question... It didn't scare him, not the way it might another man. It was out of his hands. Whatever might ultimately come was Laurel's decision. It was the simple not knowing that was gnawing at him.

It'd change everything. No fucking doubt. His life was predictable in ways he found both reassuring and monotonous, and a baby would throw it all into chaos. That wasn't to say he couldn't handle it, but it would be a far more welcome challenge a few years down the road.

Laurel, though. She had potential. He might make decent money working construction, but it was nothing like what she could pull in if she managed to land an engineering job. A *career.* That was what she needed to be worried about, right now. Plus there was her mental health. She'd gone through a long blue patch over the holidays, and at his urging got prescribed an antidepressant she could take on an as-needed basis. It seemed to be helping a lot. Would she have to give that up, if she took on a pregnancy?

He dropped the weights he'd been using onto the rack with twin clangs, swore under his breath. He needed to chill the fuck out. He eyed the handful of guys on the benches and at the heavy bags, sizing them up. All kids or newbies, nobody fit to spar with. Not the way he needed to fight right now. He went through the rest of his routine, seeking solace and not finding any. Jesus, uncertainty was the motherfucking worst.

Desperate for distraction, he went back to the grocery store, bought the ingredients for the only thing he knew how to cook that tasted any good—casserole. He cooked noodles and slices of sausage and mixed them up with marinara sauce and covered it with mozzarella and foil and stuck it in the oven just in time to leave to pick up Laurel. If she hadn't bought a test or gotten her period, they'd make a stop at Rite Aid.

He was just shrugging into his jacket when a familiar sound stilled him—a knock and the scrabble of a key in the lock.

Laurel appeared, smiling, snowflakes melting in her hair. Then that smile drooped, her eyes taking in his coat and hat. "Were you about to come get me?"

"Yeah."

"I left you a message, like, four hours ago. My coworker lives around the corner—she gave me a lift."

"Oh."

"You really need to check your phone."

"I don't think I can even get text messages."

She smirked. "You can, you just refuse to learn how. And I left you a voicemail, anyhow. I know you."

"Oops."

"Doesn't matter. I'm here now. Saved you the trip." She shed her coat and hung it up, then stepped close, rising on tiptoes to pull the cap from his head.

He kissed her temple. "How was work?"

"Exhausting. Like, really exhausting."

He didn't doubt it—she looked wiped, eyes dull and cheeks pink. Though now he thought about it, it wasn't that windy today.

"I'm making dinner."

She perked up some at that. "Are you? Let me guess—Italian casserole."

"You guess right."

"Well, good. I like your one recipe. I brought leftovers, but it's only dessert, so that's perfect."

"You don't look so hot," he said.

"Thanks very much."

"Can I get you something?"

"I dunno…" She unwound the scarf from her neck. "When's dinner?"

"An hour."

"I just want to lie down, I think. I'm all hot and woozy. I hope I don't have the flu."

How selfish is it that I hope maybe you do? If it was between that or being pregnant, he knew which one he felt prepared for. "Go lie down, then. I'll wake you up when it's ready."

Only he didn't. Laurel curled up on his bed and passed out, and he didn't wake her when the timer dinged. He took the foil off the dish and let the cheese brown, then turned the oven on low. Heather had lent him a book, some novel about broke-ass college guys in the Northwest doing rowing back in the World War II days or something. He stretched out beside Laurel on the bed and stared at the first page and kept on staring, didn't take in more than six words while he waited for her to wake.

At long last, a *hmm*, a yawn. A dozy groan and she turned onto her side, eyes blinking open to find him there.

"Dinner smells good. Is it ready?"

"It is."

"What time is it?"

He looked to the microwave. "Ten twenty-one."

"Whoa. What?"

"You were beat."

She sat up. "Jesus. I napped for three hours?"

"Hungry?"

She looked down at her stomach as though conferring. "Very."

"Good. Me too."

Beyond hungry, in Flynn's case. He'd only eaten a fistful of cheese and a few slices of sausage since before his workout. His gut was packed with butterflies, but they weren't particularly filling.

Laurel moved to the couch and he loaded a couple bowls with dried-out casserole. He made it a whole minute before the clinking of forks drove him to blurt, "You buy a pregnancy test?"

Pausing mid-chew, she studied him with still-sleepy eyes. She swallowed. "No, I didn't."

"Not to sound paranoid, but when'd you get your period last?"

She frowned, thinking. "Oh—it was New Year's morning. I remember I had a champagne hangover and that showed up on top of it."

"That was almost two months ago."

"I know, but like I said, sometimes they don't come at all on the Pill, or just a mini one."

That didn't do much to slow his pulse. "Maybe I should go out and get one now. Just so we can rule it out."

She nibbled her lip.

"Just ask me to. I don't mind." *And I'm fucking dying inside.* No news was *not* good news. Whoever'd come up with that saying was so full of shit.

"It's after ten. And it's snowing."

"Someplace'll be open. Star Market."

"What, in Dorchester?"

"Wouldn't you sleep better?" He would. He might sleep at all, in fact. "Seriously, it's no big deal. I'll get you some Nyquil while I'm at it, in case it's the flu. I'll go right now."

"Maybe..."

"I'm going," he announced, setting his bowl on the coffee table and reaching for one of his boots. "And I'll grab tampons, in case it's just PMS. And Kettle Chips."

She smiled, seeming to surrender. "You know, there's something surpassingly manly about a guy who'll pick tampons up for you without batting an eye."

"Your pussy doesn't scare me, honey."

"No, I daresay it doesn't. I could come—"

"Nope, you couldn't. Eat up. Stay warm. Back soon."

She smiled and shook her head, watching him lace his boots and pull on a hat, something simultaneously soft and fierce about her expression. Or maybe that was a fever brewing.

Twenty minutes later, Flynn was unloading his basket onto the checkout conveyer belt. The young clerk passed his purchases stoically across the scanner—tampons, Nyquil, potato chips, pregnancy test, plus a bottle of red wine. It wasn't until he handed over the plastic bag that the kid showed any sign of life, saying flatly, "Party time."

Flynn was tempted to meet the snark with a verbal backhand, but he didn't have it in him just now. Instead he muttered, "You know it," and headed for the door.

Pregnant. Pregnant. The word had grown larger and larger over the course of the drive, thundering now, echoing and huge. He let it tumble around his skull as he started the trip back home, windshield wipers batting harmless fluffy flakes aside.

What if she *was* pregnant? He'd been preoccupied with the thought all day, but it changed now, with the test in his possession. With an actual answer at hand.

Plus that's not really the question, is it?

The real question for Flynn was, what would she want to do about it if she was?

It wasn't his decision, but if she asked what *he* wanted her to do… Shit, be honest? Or refuse to say so she wouldn't feel pressured? But refusing to say, was that supporting her choice or was that forcing her to make it completely on her own? He thought he knew what he'd want her to do, but it felt so goddamn delicate, the question of whether or not to say.

She might not be pregnant. Probably isn't. Some cramps and hot flashes could be anything, and feeling exhausted after waitressing all day was to be expected. The female body was like a car with no manual, a mystery designed to confound and bewitch the simple male brain. A man was lucky to get invited to dick around under the hood and go for a spin, but fuck if any of them knew how to service the thing.

He pulled up behind his building, yellow streetlight making the steadily fattening snowflakes glow like gold. The plastic bag felt monumental in his grip, as though he were lugging a bomb, not a couple pounds of snacks and feminine hygiene products.

Not a bomb, he corrected. A pregnancy was scary and profound and life-altering, but that was a metaphor too far. Still, his hand was shaking unmistakably as he unlocked the door.

"Honey, I'm home. Got you booze and chips and a stick for peeing on. You on the rag yet?"

A laugh answered that crass greeting, loosening his chest, if only by a fraction. "No, I am not."

He flipped the deadbolt, rummaged in the bag and pitched the box toward the bed where she was lounging. "Best pee on a stick then, woman."

She'd changed into her pajamas—or rather, her pajama bottoms and one of his tee shirts. Why was that so fucking sexy? Though he was grateful to register any reaction apart from anxiety, he set the thought aside. *Answers first, then depravity. We can fuck to celebrate, if it's negative.*

Laurel knelt and picked up the box, studying it. She opened it while Flynn peeled off his layers.

"Thanks for doing this." She unfolded the instructions. "Going out in that."

"It was nothing. Go pee on a stick," he repeated.

"The snow's picking up," she said, still reading.

"Go pee on a stick."

She met his eyes, smiled dryly. "I guess I'll go pee on a stick, then."

"What a good idea. How long does it take to get the answer?"

She scanned the paper. "Three minutes. Wow, that sounds really fast and like forever at the same time."

Well put. "There's chips and wine, while you wait."

She smiled. "Classy. If it comes back a plus sign I better spit the booze out, huh?"

There was a joke in there, but he barely heard it, caught too completely on *plus sign*. Plus sign. How could one shape—two fucking little perpendicular lines—possibly be so powerful?

Then he thought of the cross, that symbol that had dominated his childhood and bullied his psyche, and somehow it made perfect sense.

Fuck you, lines.

At least these lines would bring answers. The other kind had done nothing but torment and confuse and contradict.

Right. Now, to survive the longest three minutes of his entire life.

CHAPTER FIVE

LAUREL CREPT OUT OF THE BATHROOM practically on tiptoes, paranoid any sudden movement might somehow queer the test.

Flynn was planted at the edge of the mattress, hands clasped between his knees. "Well?"

"I just did it. Two minutes to go, probably." She wished she hadn't done the dishes already. A chore would be a welcome distraction.

"That took ages."

"I know." She flopped down beside him, splaying her hands on her belly and staring up at the ceiling. "I read the instructions, like, eight times. If we only had the one test, I wasn't looking to send you back out in the snow."

"How hard can it be? 'Step one, pee on stick.'"

She let her arm fall back behind her, smacking his side. "It's trickier than that. You have to angle it and stuff, and pee for just the right amount of time."

"Good thing you're an engineer."

She shot him a look. "Are you being mean to me?"

"No, sorry. Not on purpose. Fuck, I'm fucking nervous."

Laurel softened. "Me too." She sat up and circled a hand over his back. "Have you ever done this before?"

"No."

"I swear I've been taking the pills correctly."

"I believe you. You won't even let the toilet paper hang facing the wall—no way you'd get sloppy about that sort of thing."

"It'll probably be negative. The chances are really low."

"Maybe I have, like, stealthy-ass fuckin' Jason Bourne sperm that snuck by your defenses."

She snorted. "My uterus isn't a Swiss bank. It doesn't work like that, anyhow. It suppresses eggs from being released."

"My sperm are so powerful your eggs couldn't resist them."

"My God, if it's positive you're going to be insufferable, aren't you?"

"Maybe. After I regain consciousness. Think it's been three minutes?"

Her hand stilled. "Yeah. But I'm too scared to check."

"I could. One line is negative and a plus sign is knocked up, right?"

"No, no. I'll go." She sat up, looked at him long and hard.

He must have sensed the time for joking was over; he took her hand and gave it a squeeze. "I can go with you."

She pursed her lips. It all felt so insanely intimate, this moment. Whatever the verdict might be, she didn't yet know what she'd feel about it. Though she did know one thing. "I'll go by myself. I'd prefer you hear the news from me, rather than from staring at a stick I peed on."

"Whatever you need."

She took a deep breath, blew it out slow and noisy and didn't feel a jot calmer.

Flynn offered another squeeze and nodded toward the bathroom.

"Right. Okay. Here I go." Her hand fell from his and she crossed the small apartment, the journey at once endless and way, way too short. When she hit the switch, the light was so bright, the fan so loud. The tub so white and the tile so cold. The plastic wand sat on the sink's edge, so innocuous. She crept up on it, squinting so she couldn't make out its little window. When she had it in hand, she shut her eyes, took a breath, another, another. Opened them.

It took a moment to make sense of it. A blue line. Another blue line, fainter, crisscrossing the first, the point where they met darkest of all, like stripes intersecting on a field of gingham.

"Plus sign," she muttered. *That means pregnant. Doesn't it?* She set the wand down with a trembling hand and fished the instructions from the trash can. The illustration left no room for doubt.

Holy fuck. I'm pregnant. She snatched up the stick and stared at the window, expecting the second line to be lighter, maybe negligible, maybe inconclusive. But no, there was no denying it.

"Fuck." She glanced down at her belly, eased up the hem of her shirt. Same pasty white skin as always, same navel with the same single freckle beside it. How could this landscape look so normal, and yet something so monumental be taking place just an inch or two below the surface?

"Laurel?"

She looked to the door. "Be right out." Staring in the mirror, she found herself only wide-eyed, looking drunk or high or dazed. At a loss, she sputtered her lips in a raspberry and finger-combed her hair.

Time to change a man's life forever.

She left the bathroom. Flynn was sitting in the same spot on the bed, eyes nailed to her as she emerged. His brows rose but he said nothing.

She didn't know what to say herself. It wasn't as though they'd been trying for this. She couldn't rush him, pee-stick in hand, tossing herself into his arms and making his dreams come true.

Her silence seemed to speak for her.

"It's positive, isn't it?" he asked, voice soft and serious. Not grave, but somber, she thought.

She nodded.

"C'mere."

He took her wrist as she drew close and pulled her down onto his lap. Strong arms encircled her waist and hugged her tight, and he pressed his mouth to her throat. His exhalation was long and warm and heavy.

"What do you think?" she whispered, wishing she knew her own answer to the question.

"I don't know."

"I have no idea what to do—" She'd nearly said, *what to do about it,* but that sounded so cold, like it was a pest and she had to choose between squashing it or trapping it with a glass and an envelope and shunting it out the window.

"Two choices," Flynn said, lips tickling her neck.

"Two really awful choices. Oh. Three, I guess."

He pulled back to meet her eyes. "Three? You mean adoption?"

She nodded.

His smile was small, a mix of sad and mischievous. "Honey, if you decide to have this baby, I'm raisin' it, whether you want to join me or not."

She could only stare at him.

"That's not to say that it isn't completely your decision to make. And whatever you decide, I'll support you. But I know what it was like, having my dad walk out of my life, and no child born into this world with me as its father is gonna find out what that feels like."

She didn't know what to say to that. She doubted she could form words, anyhow, emotion lodged like a fist in her throat. Flynn's expression was soft but those eyes shone with something she knew well both from fight nights and from sex. Something hard and male and unbreakable.

"If you're not ready to be a mom," he said, "I get that. You have plans. Ones you put on hold long enough."

"Yeah. I do." She didn't want to have a child now, not before she put her degree to use, landed a job with a salary capable of even making parenthood feasible. Boston was no place to raise a kid on tips. She needed a career, and a chance to live with this man for a while, as a couple—

"Honey, you okay?"

She blinked, slipping free from the swirl of panic. He must have seen it on her face. "I'm okay. Just overwhelmed."

"We can talk about it for ages, still," he said. "For weeks, probably, right? Until you have to make a decision?"

She wasn't sure how long you could wait before getting an abortion, but she guessed she was only five weeks along, so there was time, probably. Although *time* sounded suffocating, same as the choices. "I've got a while, I guess… You'd really raise a kid on your own, if I decided I wasn't ready?"

"If the choice was that or adoption, yeah. I would."

"That'd be so hard."

"It would. But Heather managed it."

"I can't imagine what…" She trailed off, lost all over again. What on earth would the kid think of her if she walked away, left it all in Flynn's hands? To imagine saddling a child with the pain and resentment she felt toward her own mother opened up a pit in her stomach, raw and aching. She put her hand to the spot then quickly moved it away, remembering what was going on in there.

Would leaving it in his hands really be so bad, if the alternative was subjecting it to an unfit mother? A depressive, thoroughly not-ready mother? She couldn't even seem to get her professional life in order. How the fuck was she qualified to raise a child?

"You'd be okay if I decided I wasn't ready, period?" she asked.

"Completely."

But could he be? If he knew already he'd be willing to take the responsibility on by himself, did that leave room for ambivalence? Did it leave room in his heart to keep loving a woman who might choose to end the pregnancy? Was it even okay, she wondered, to be so completely clueless about what she wanted to do? Both choices made her sick to her stomach.

"I wish I felt as certain as you seem to," she whispered.

He laughed faintly. "Honey, I'm as lost as you."

"You promise?"

She felt him nodding, his chin brushing her temple. "I've felt more lost, though," he said. "Like after Robbie died, and after my dad walked out. I might be sure of what I'd do if you decided to have it, but my certainty ends there. Trust me."

"Okay." She wanted to believe that was true, but maybe he was only saying it so she wouldn't feel pressured.

"There's no way we're gonna feel any more sure about what to do before bedtime," he said.

"No, definitely not."

"What should we do, then? Movie?"

"Maybe." She wouldn't take in a second of it and she doubted Flynn would either, but it sounded like a comforting farce. She left his lap to cross the room and open her bag, pulled out her computer. He didn't own a TV, so they watched things in bed, the laptop propped on a milk crate between their feet. Half the time they just wound up messing around, but for some reason they never sat on the couch.

"I brought cheesecake back from work," she said. "You want any?"

"Nah. Maybe for breakfast."

Probably wise. Her stomach was a merry-go-round.

One with a single tiny rider. Jesus Christ.

"What movie?" she asked, voice half-breaking.

"You pick. No superheroes." He headed for the bathroom. He'd no doubt find and study the pee-wand still sitting on the sink.

Laurel grabbed the milk crate and set up their makeshift entertainment center, sitting cross-legged before the screen. She scrolled and scrolled, finding little of interest. In truth, in no universe was there any movie half as engrossing as the unexpected drama currently unfolding in her middle.

In the end she settled on some generic action movie, cueing it up, waiting for Flynn. She left the bed, intending to get herself a glass of wine, then promptly sat down, realizing her drinking days were done until such time as she knew what her choice was going to be. It triggered fresh panic, to think she had to get through the immediate future without the aid of alcohol. And the fact that that panicked her panicked her further.

How the fuck can I have a baby? I'm not even sure if I have a drinking problem or not.

Plus there was her depression. Did that make postpartum depression a greater likelihood? She didn't even need to wonder if having a depressed parent could hurt a kid—that was the story of her life. Plus the kid could inherit those same struggles, or Flynn's anxiety, or her mom's shit, or all of the above.

Flynn finally reappeared. He'd taken so long she wondered if he too had gotten caught up re-re-re-reading the test's instructions and staring at the faint blue line.

"What kept you?" she asked, mustering a teasing smile.

"Just starin' at a plus sign until my eyes crossed."

"I guessed right."

"What're we watching?"

"We're going to pretend to watch some movie about a hit man. But I imagine we'll both be thoroughly stuck in our own heads."

He nodded, opening a dresser drawer and pulling out some pajama bottoms and a clean thermal. Laurel watched him change, admiring his body with a reverent strain of appreciation. She was lost in biology just now, awed by Flynn in a way that had nothing and everything to do with sex.

His child is growing inside me. Perhaps a dream come true five or more years down the road, but for now, the most confounding decision of her life.

They went through the usual ritual, Laurel hitting PLAY and the two of them propping pillows up against the shelves behind the bed, sitting side by side, her leaning into him, chilly feet finding each other beneath the covers. Usually she had a glass or bottle of something in her hand at times like this, and there it was again—that guilty pang to register how much she wanted a drink right now.

Her hand sought his atop the covers, and she took comfort in the size of it, the familiarity. She didn't trust her intuition. It had become a close friend in the past half a year, but right now it felt like a broken Magic 8-Ball. Like she might ask it what to do, but all she'd get back was blue liquid pooling in her lap and the rattle of plastic inside plastic. Or perhaps simply, *Reply hazy. Try again.* And again, and again, every answer the same, identically unhelpful.

For half an hour they each pretended to give the movie their full attention, Laurel lost in what-ifs and certain Flynn was equally preoccupied.

She squeezed his hand before letting it go. "Need the bathroom."

"Pause it."

"Nah, I'm fine." She had no clue who any of the characters were or what they were up to, and wasn't interested in finding out.

When she returned, Flynn had tossed the covers aside, sitting with his legs outstretched in a V—a familiar invitation. She climbed onto the bed and got settled before him, grateful for his warm chest at her back, his strong arms circling her middle. She pulled the blanket back over them and laid her hands atop his in her lap.

"You taking any of this in?" he asked.

"Not a single pixel. What are you thinking about?"

"Blue lines. You?"

"Mainly marveling how I can have absolutely no idea what the right decision is supposed to be."

"You've got time," he reminded her.

We, she wanted to correct him. *We've got time.* It felt scary and lonely having the choice shoved wholly into her lap. She wanted to resent him for it, but she knew where his insistence was coming from. It was always the woman's choice, ultimately. Though fuck, that was a shitload of responsibility.

"It'd be easier if you were an asshole," she said.

"Oh?"

"It's obvious what decision would be best for me—this is the exact worst time possible for me to have a child. But if I could also say it'd be shitty for the kid, it'd make it all so easy. But I'm pretty sure you'd be a great father, so really, deciding to end it sounds completely selfish."

"Not completely. It's not easy growing up with a single parent. Or with two parents, if one of them isn't up for it. I think you'd do a great job, don't get me wrong, but I also think you'd do a better job if you were ready."

"Mm."

"You count, Laurel. What's best for you matters. I know your own mom didn't do much to drive that home, but it's true."

She felt emotion rush and rise at that, something breaking free in her chest, making her eyes sting. "How would you feel if I ended it? Disappointed or relieved?"

"I dunno. Maybe I'll find out, and maybe I won't."

She sighed, exasperated and exhausted.

"I won't tell you what you should do," he said sternly. "I'll do everything I can to help you figure it out—we can talk about it 'til we're hoarse. But I dunno what I want any more than you do. I only know what I'd do if you decided to keep it, which is stick around."

She frowned, stumbling over a question she'd never thought to ask him in all their months together. "Do you *want* children? Like, theoretically. Not even with me, specifically, just in general. Do you want kids?"

"I think so."

She craned her neck to meet his eyes. "Yeah?"

"Probably. I'm kinda on the fence, always have been. Some days kids seem great, like they'd make life have a bigger purpose or whatever. Other days it sounds like hell and I can't figure out why anyone would want any. I think if I didn't have any, I'd always wonder if I was missing out, always wonder if I woulda been a decent dad. But I don't think I'd regret it, necessarily. What about you? You want kids?"

"I think maybe. I mean, my gut says I would like one, in ten years or something, but then you do the math and ten years from now my eggs'll be all dried up and dusty."

She felt him laugh, a silent shimmy of his chest at her back.

"But imagining having a baby *five* years from now?" she said. "I know I'd be thirty-five and that's already kinda pushing it, but that sounds so *soon*. Fuck, I dunno. Maybe I'd feel different if I was using my degree. Or was married. Or basically did any of this shit in the right order."

"Sure."

"Maybe I'll wake up tomorrow and the answer will be so obvious..."

"Maybe."

"But probably not."

He gave her a hug and the sweet, clumsy weight of his chin came to rest on the crown of her head.

"Tell me what to do," she murmured.

"Nope."

"I feel so alone in this."

"Your body, your choice."

She rolled her eyes, sighed her annoyance.

"Still think feminism's not complicated?"

"Shut up, Flynn."

He laughed.

"'My body, my choice'—that's about the right to have an abortion, not about women being the ones who have to make the decision for a couple."

"This little clump of tissue or whatever it looks like—if you decided to turn it into a baby—is going to have a bigger impact on your life than mine. It'd derail your career for the next couple years *at least*. It'd force you to figure out how serious you are about me, and probably sooner than you planned to."

"Sure." She hadn't thought of that. She was stupid in love with Flynn, but that wasn't the same as being ready to marry him. They made each other happy, here in these early months of new attraction and sexual exploration, but that couldn't compare to living with someone for two or three years. She wanted to know how they'd be when the honeymoon lust mellowed to something more companionable. More than that, she wanted to be able to enjoy that shift, with only the relationship at stake.

But my body seems ready. And there's no other man I'd want to leap into the terrifying unknown with. Plus Flynn really would be a great father. No doubt strict and a little controlling, but fierce and loving, too.

Fuck, she had no clue. But having him at her back, literally in this moment and in whatever decision she decided was best for her, she felt strong, if still uncertain. He was the only one she could imagine being this lost with.

She turned in his arms, draping her legs over his thigh and putting her hand to his jaw. It was Sunday night and he was as stubbly as he ever got, and she admired the rough bristle of it, of this tiny little taste of letting go from a man who gripped the reins of his life so tightly.

"What?" he asked, voice so soft the movie all but swallowed it.

"Just admiring you."

"Thought you were annoyed with me."

She smiled. "Never for long. Thank you, Flynn. For being so calm about this. I know a lot of guys would be losing their minds."

"Who says I'm not?"

She studied his eyes, shook her head. "Nope, no freak-outs hiding in there."

"Maybe not any freak-outs. But my brain's goin' a mile a minute."

She looked to his chest, traced the little triangle hem at the center of his thermal's collar. "We got thwarted this morning."

"We did."

"You want to pick up where we left off?"

He laughed. "You want to fuck?"

"I think so, yeah."

He moved, above her in a blink, cupped hand guiding her head to a pillow.

"Well," he said, and kissed her softly, "I hope you feel like getting fucked for six hours, because I can't remember the last time I was this distracted."

She laughed. "Maybe five and a half."

Flynn slapped the laptop shut and moved it aside, and they shed their clothes between deepening kisses.

Laurel searched for signs that it was different this time. It didn't feel heavy or angsty. It didn't feel monumental, but it didn't feel like usual, either. There was something delicate—no, not delicate. Vulnerable. There was something *vulnerable* in the way they touched and the way he watched as she slicked herself with lube. Something even akin to fascination, his eyes narrowed as though he were seeing her in some new and remarkable light.

Or maybe that was just hormones.

"Ready?" he asked.

She nodded.

He sank deep, slowly. No cramps met the intrusion and she stroked his neck and his hair, sighed her pleasure. He dropped low, resting his forehead against hers and merely holding there for a time, that wild body tame and patient. She let her hands wander his chest and ribs to settle on his hips, and she tugged.

He gave her his cock in smooth, steady strokes, silent at first, until a soft shudder of a moan filled the air between them. She shivered, melting, pussy welcoming him deep.

As he found a pace she studied his face, the tendons in his neck, the shapes of his chest and arms, a rush of startling clarity making it feel as though they were standing in the broad light of day. *This is a man who would absolutely defend and protect my child.* The truth of that thought struck her in a deep, visceral place, vibrating on a wholly animal wavelength.

She changed beneath him, hands gripping him tight, thighs hugging his hips, urging him to go faster, deeper, to make it rougher. Not so much as a twinge this time.

"Feel okay?" he whispered.

"I need you."

"You get me."

"Harder."

"How hard?"

"Ninety percent." They spoke of his capacity for harshness in percentages sometimes, a hundred equaling the way he got when they role-played. Tonight she wanted his strength and aggression, but no playacting. Brash possession, and a chance to wallow in it as his lover, not his victim.

He pressed hard into her, forcing her legs wide and making her feel the obscene weight of his body. Something lit up inside her, feeling his power. She hadn't had a chance to wonder how the pregnancy might change his attraction to her, if he'd still be comfortable being this way, being rough. She'd hate to feel as though she couldn't be what he needed, couldn't grant his darkest wishes. It deepened that ravenous sensation inside her, curled her fingers into claws against his skin and had her breath coming in gruff gasps.

She raked her nails up and down his back. "You feel so good."

"You like me deep?"

"Yeah."

"Need it faster? Slower?"

"Faster."

He gave her that, their bodies meeting with sharp smacks. "Touch yourself."

"Not yet. I want to go crazy first." A couple times she'd come from nothing more than the fucking, but nearly always she needed her clit touched. Until then, the thrust of his cock was an exquisite tease and she lost herself in the friction, the slide and thrust, the impact of his hips. More even than the physical stimulation, his voice was setting her on fire. His exhalations were rhythmic grunts, soon lengthening to moans.

"Fuck me," she whispered, mouth right at his ear.

"Take my cock, girl."

Girl. Not honey, now. He was slipping deeper into his kink, and she welcomed the shift.

"Get on top," he ordered.

He moved to sit and she straddled him, feeling his guiding fist as her sex sought his cock then claimed it, deep.

"Yeah. Ride me."

She sat up and leaned back, adjusting until she had the right angle. She took him smooth and slow, feeling magnetic with those blue eyes watching every undulation. All that wildness she objectified in him, it was coursing through her now. She felt powerful and ferocious, owning this man, and as not a single drop of wine had been drunk, she couldn't blame her brazenness on alcohol. This was something even stronger, something mammalian and ancient and hot as sin.

He looked hypnotized, lost in the spell her body was casting. Her excitement mounted, gathering deep and low against the slick friction. She'd only come a couple of times this way, without touching her clit, and it had turned her inside-out.

"Lay back."

He did and she dropped to her palms, seeking the right pressure, chasing that hot, angry hum in her cunt. Her eyes roamed his skin, the faint sheen of sweat on his clenched abdomen, the knitting of muscle between his pecs and along his ribs. All at once her hips were driving, this sex feeling like an out-of-body experience.

His gaze was electric, nailed between them. "Yeah, use that dick. Fuck me."

She buried her face against his neck. "You feel so good."

"Love the way you fuck me, honey."

Honey. So close. "Say my name."

"Laurel."

Pleasure burst open inside her. "Yeah."

"You gonna come on me?"

She nodded, eyes squeezed shut, lips pressed to his throat. She tried to say yes, to say his name back, to say anything, but all that came was a mewling, frightened yelp of a moan, as all at once she was bearing down on release.

"Yeah, come on my dick. Use me, Laurel."

She did. He was everything—a hard cock, a gorgeous body, the man who shocked and comforted and irked and supported her, all of it feeling so starkly plain, sweet and bestial, at once a Valentine and pornography. The pleasure spiked, leveled, spiked, leveled, and she chased the orgasm so hard she thought her hips might seize up, but then—

"Oh God. Oh God."

"Come on, honey. Do it."

She already was. A shrieking, shuddering possession of a climax, like the kind she got through her clit, only tripled. Time slipped away as she rode the sensations—more a bucking bronco than a soothing ocean tide—and she didn't know what she said, what he said in return. She was aware only of their bodies and, in time, the feel of his arm in her grip, and the sight of his skin beneath her raking nails. She pulled her hand back, half expecting blood. But no, merely marks.

"Jesus."

He smiled, looking so amused and so patient, sprawled beneath her. "Good?"

"Crazy."

"Glad to hear it. Turn over."

She did, legs like noodles. He pushed inside, gruff, one hand on her hip and the other splayed across her lower back. In seconds flat it was rough again, so right and essential. With every thrust he tugged her hard to him, feeling ten feet tall behind her, unspeakably strong. She wanted more of him, more of every fucking thing about this man.

She arched her back. "Hold my hair."

He gathered it in a fist.

"Yeah."

"You need another?"

"I won't be greedy."

"Bullshit. You take what you want." *If men could have multiple orgasms,* he'd said once, *sex would take a fucking week.*

"Touch me, then," she said. Unwilling to give up that cruel hand in her hair, she rose up on her knees. She held her breath, waiting until she felt those rough fingertips on her clit, the contact like a whip crack.

"Light," she panted. "Light, to start."

"Love when you get bossy," he teased, hips punishing.

He gave her exactly what she needed—the barest whisper of friction at first, then a little quicker, a little more pressure as her nerves recovered. She got lost in the feel of his body owning hers— his hard belly against her ass, the filthy, exquisite intrusion of his cock. Got lost in the mean tug of his grip in her hair and the deft caresses of his fingers on her clit.

She came hard and deep, groaning. His fingers kept on stroking, cock still pounding, and just when she thought the sensation was going to rip her apart, another climax tore through her. She came down from it reeling and sweating and shaking, feeling high. Feeling crazed. She dropped to her hands and knees, muscles spent.

"Now," he murmured, sounding full of himself, "it's my turn."

Those cruel hands claimed her hips, holding her in place as he took his pleasure. She craned her neck for a glimpse of his face. She wanted to drown in that expression, so determined and haughty but desperate behind it all.

This sex felt different. She hadn't been in her head the way she usually was. Hadn't needed any tangible thoughts to spur her pleasure, hadn't wasted a second on insecurities. She'd been a thousand percent locked in her body and connected to his. Possibly the most primal sex of her life.

And why wouldn't it be? Fraught as their situation was, the biological fact of his would-be child inside her coursed like a drug, like the madness of ovulation times ten.

Behind her, he was coming undone. His thrusts raced and their rhythm faltered; she felt his hands trembling on her hips.

"Fuck, honey." One palm left her, only to come down on her ass, making her jump and gasp. The spot flared hot and then he was rubbing at it, easing the sting. He pushed her down with his weight and Laurel lay flat on her belly with one cheek on the covers, brought her legs tight together when his knees urged her to. He braced his forearms beside her shoulders, his frantic body spilling heat and sound, feeling like the entire world.

He came with a thundering moan, pressing close, driving deep, falling still and silent after three long, clenching thrusts.

She listened to his breathing, the delicious rush and gasp of his disbelief and satisfaction. She hummed a happy sound, smiling.

"Mm." He kissed her cheek, squeezed her tightly with his arms and legs. His cock was going soft, slipping from her along with the warm spoils of their sex.

"Turn over," he said again.

Laurel rolled onto her back and he grabbed a washcloth from the little plastic bin on the shelf where the lube—and formerly the condoms—lived. She tidied herself and he lay beside her. She watched his ribs rise and fall, rise and fall, and breathed them both in.

"No cramps, huh?"

She dropped the towel over the edge of the bed. "Nope."

He turned onto his side, propping himself up on his elbow. "Is it just me, or was that fucking intense?"

"It's not just you." She glowed to know he'd felt the same way. Pleased to imagine it had felt even a fraction as mind-altering to him as it had to her. "That was like... I was going to say an out-of-body experience, but actually I mean the opposite. Like my brain checked out and my body was... I dunno, but it was crazy. Crazy hot. Crazy good."

"That's what I like to hear."

"Maybe your pheromones are, like, turbo-charged, because of…you know."

"Maybe I'm just fuckin' great in the sack."

She rolled her eyes and tapped his chin and lips with a clumsy finger. He kissed it, then caught it between his lips, suckling. She smiled, charmed and spent and blissed out beyond reason.

"I propose we fall asleep ASAP," she said, "to maximize the orgasm haze and minimize the chance of lying awake and thinking too hard about stuff."

"There'll be plenty of time for that tomorrow."

She nodded, mushing her hair into the tangled covers. "My thoughts exactly."

"You go first," he said, meaning the bathroom.

She took the invitation, padding naked through the apartment. Strangely, she didn't feel cold at all. At least not until she stepped into the bright and whirring bathroom, only to spot the fateful pee-wand on the sink's edge.

Still a plus sign. Still a hell of a question, demanding a fuck of an answer. Just like that, the haze was gone, sucked away by the shower fan. And Laurel knew she'd be lucky to sleep a single wink, tonight.

CHAPTER SIX

"Now you're *definitely* sure about this?"

Flynn glanced at the girl in his passenger seat—a year or two younger than Laurel, plump, with a plain, expressive face and a vinyl purse shaped like a cheeseburger.

"Positive," he said.

It had been a week since the appearance of the little blue plus sign, and whether Laurel's roommate knew she was pregnant, Flynn wasn't sure. He doubted it. Laurel held things back, held things in, even from her friends. Plus Anne hadn't said anything to suggest she knew, and unlike Laurel, she *wasn't* the type to withhold.

Anyhow, this mission had to do with a different—if no less monumental—uncertainty.

"This is *so* exciting," Anne said, shaking her mittened fists before her, all but vibrating. "I'm so honored you tapped me for the job."

"I'm relieved as fuck you said yes. I don't have the first clue what sort of a ring she'd want."

Nor did Flynn have the first clue if Laurel would say yes when he proposed. He only knew that *he* was certain, and ready, and that the decision felt right.

They'd been living with the unanswered question of the pregnancy for what felt like eons, and though he ached for a decision, he knew better than to rush her. Plus he felt nearly comfortable with the ambiguity, now. And steeled more than ever in his commitment, whether they wound up raising a kid together in nine months or five years or never. His mind was made up, and he'd always defaulted to action over navel-gazing.

At this very moment, Laurel was at his sister's place, helping get ready for a party to celebrate his niece's graduation from vocational college. It was a Sunday and he'd told Laurel a white lie—said he'd picked up an overtime shift for the afternoon and that he'd catch up with them all later. No doubt with a tiny velvet box burning a hole in his jacket pocket.

"You came to the right woman," Anne said with gravity.

"You sound confident."

"I bet Laurel and I have watched the past four *Bachelor* and *Bachelorette* finales together."

"That a TV show?"

"It is! It's the best TV show there is. And at the end of every season a chick gets proposed to, and there's always a bit where the dude—or dudes—pick out the engagement ring. They show them perusing a few different designs, and we judge the crap out of every one."

"So what's she into? Laurel?"

"Simple, for sure. Anytime they show a ring with loads of crap on it she's all, like, 'Gross.' So definitely a solitaire, or *maybe* a solitaire plus a couple tiny diamonds on the sides. But not slathered in gaudy diamond frosting, you know?"

"All right. So gold, or…?"

"Have you *ever* seen Laurel wear gold jewelry?"

He frowned, drawing a blank. "I have no idea."

Anne shook her head in his periphery. "You're such a guy."

"What gave me away?"

"She's a silver girl, all the way. So that means either white gold or platinum. Whichever your budget can handle."

"I figured it was most important to get her the biggest diamond I can afford." He wasn't rolling in it, but he lived simply and worked hard and had a respectable hunk of savings to his name; you had to when you didn't boast some cushy gig with a 401K.

"Don't get anything gigantic," Anne said. "It has to fit a woman's frame."

"Her frame?"

"Oh my God, you're so lucky I'm here."

"Clearly."

"Plus you can get a *big* diamond, but one with some flaws in it, for the same price as a smaller one that's closer to perfect."

"Oh." Shit, there was more to this than he'd realized. Better to have Anne explain than get taken for a ride by the salesperson. Like the opposite of Flynn taking his sister's car to the shop for her.

"Personally, I'd say go somewhere in the middle. A little flaw or two is fine. I mean, it's not like people walk around wearing jewelers' monocles, right?"

"Right." A jeweler's what now?

"And it has to be a conflict-free diamond, obviously."

"Obviously." Crickets chirped between his ears.

"What shape, do you think?" Anne talked a mile a minute, but today Flynn welcomed it. It didn't allow his own nervous mental commentary to get a word in edgewise, even if these questions had him feeling less prepared by the minute.

"Shape? They're just, like, round, aren't they?"

"Usually. But there's loads of other options too. Square and oval and marquis and emerald and radiant—oh, radiant is *really* classy."

"Jesus, am I qualified for this? I've only got a high school diploma."

"I'll hold your gigantic hand. Have you guys talked about marriage much?"

"Not…explicitly," he said. Not at all, in fact. He'd made the mistake of teasing Laurel about it way back when they'd first been hooking up, and it had weirded her out so much he'd not dared mention the M-word since.

"So this is going to be a complete surprise."

"Pretty much."

"Why now?"

He kept his eyes glued to the road through the watery flakes pelting the windshield. "It just hit me." Like a fist to the face. And he'd recovered from the resulting daze without a doubt in his mind.

"You know how you're going to propose?"

"Not really." Again, not at all.

"When?"

"Not sure. When it feels right." In the next week or two, he imagined, some time when it was just the two of them. Before she decided about the pregnancy, he hoped. He wanted her to know where he stood. Wanted her to know that if she kept it, he was in this. And that if she didn't, it didn't change how he felt for her, how serious he was… Though now he thought about it, maybe it would make her decision harder, if he proposed first. Maybe that was too much pressure, like a big fat sign she'd take to mean he wanted her to have the baby.

And is it? Fuck if he even knew—

"You nervous?"

He cracked a smile. "Terrified."

"Ha! This from the guy who volunteers to get assaulted every weekend. For free." Anne had come along to the fights with Laurel once and spent the entire night wincing and shielding her eyes with her purse. "For *free*," she said again, throwing her pink wooly hands up in disbelief.

"For fun."

"You know what's super fun? Bar trivia. Badminton. Getting drunk and trying on all the clothes in your closet."

"Your closet, maybe." He exited the highway, taking them onto a neglected route trimmed with tired strip malls. When they reached the plaza, he was relieved to see the jewelry store was nicer-looking than most of its neighbors. He parked and shut off the engine, sat holding the wheel and staring blankly between his fists.

Anne patted his shoulder. "Nothing to fear, champ. Just a massively expensive purchase with no guarantee she'll say yes."

"When you put it that way."

"C'mon. Let's go look at sparkly shit."

And since the car was getting cold, he flung his door open and took the next big, icy step into the unknown.

* * *

"How's this?" Laurel asked, holding up a sugar cookie to show Flynn's sister.

Heather eyed it in her beady way and nodded. "Perfect."

Before them on the kitchen table were tubes of icing and sprinkles and those little silver balls that just had to be poisonous, Laurel imagined. The cookies were supposed to be snowflakes, frosted pale blue and white, but they'd spread a bit in the oven and given the color scheme, they could've passed for trussed-up Stars of David.

She set the test cookie aside and got to work on the rest while Heather layered a lasagna. For a family named Flynn they certainly did lean heavily on Italian bakes. Then again, she'd never before had a meal at Heather's not bestowed by a surly delivery driver, so it felt very fancy indeed.

For Laurel, the afternoon was a welcome break from the lingering questions that nagged at her day and night. A week since she'd peed on that stick—and two days since she'd peed on a second one, also positive—and she felt no closer to confident about her decision. But for the next few hours, it wasn't about her. It was about Kim, and about cookies, and fun and celebration. She just hoped no one noticed her toasting with seltzer water.

The young woman of the hour was out at the moment picking up her daughter from her ex's mom's house, leaving just Laurel and Heather to handle the party prep. Once upon a time this apartment had seemed so harsh and unwelcoming to Laurel, with its cigarette undertones and the incessant drone of the portable TV on the kitchen counter, always tuned to court TV or trashy talk shows.

Heather herself had initially intimidated the crap out of Laurel, as well. She was nearly fifteen years older than Flynn, an abrasive South Boston native with a lanky build and a hulking presence, a load of auburn hair and clashing roots and no deficit of eye shadow. Everything about Heather Flynn growled, *Don't fuck with me,* but Laurel had grown very fond of her. She'd stepped up to raise her brother in her twenties and was every inch the mama bulldog, but she hid a heart of gold behind the sandpaper veneer.

Her daughter Kim had just completed a certificate program in medical billing. The family, broken though it was, was fiery and proud, and you'd think Kim had just graduated from Harvard with honors.

Laurel, on the other hand, had had no one cheering when she'd crossed the stage to accept her Bachelor's in Engineering at Wentworth aside from her classmates, to say nothing of a party to mark the occasion. The whole thing struck her as slightly outlandish but infinitely charming, and she envied Kim, she could admit. Or perhaps it merely humbled her to remember how she'd judged Flynn's niece when they'd first met, thinking she was a sulky, overgrown teenager who'd had a kid way too young and fucked up her life.

Joke's on me, Laurel thought. In no time at all Kim might land a job that paid better than Laurel's waitressing gig. The engineering market in Boston was tight and competitive, and it didn't help that she'd let her education lapse. She wanted to kick herself, some days. Now more than ever.

"You're quiet." Heather's accent was as heavy as her brother's. *Yaw quiet.*

"Am I normally noisy?" Laurel deflected, knowing full well Heather had her pegged.

"Somethin's on your mind."

Laurel went with the truth, if not the one that really had her preoccupied. "Just thinking about how Kim's getting her shit together, and here I am, officially thirty, and no closer to a career than I was when I was her age. Makes me realize a Bachelor's is just a waste of time and money if you're too much of a coward to use it."

"It's not too late."

"I know," she said, pressing a silver bauble into the center of a blue cookie. "It just looks so bad to potential employers, that I've let it get so moldy."

"Just keep at it. It's all well and good kickin' your own ass if it gets you movin', but don't pause long enough to let the self-pity take root. Trust me, I'm Catholic. I know guilt. And guilt gets shit *done*."

"No, I know. And you're right. For me, inaction is the absolute worst thing. If I think too hard about it, I get scared. And if I get scared, I clam up. It's just such a slog, sending out résumé after résumé and getting nothing back. Like I'm shouting into the— Oh."

Pain spread through her lower back, slow and intense, as though her tailbone were in a vise. "Oh. *Oh*, Jesus."

Heather glanced up, cheese bag in hand. "You okay?"

"It's my back." She clutched the spot, rubbing, not caring if she was getting frosting on her sweater.

"You throw it out?"

Laurel shook her head, gnashed her teeth through a fresh, mean wave of agony. "No," she groaned. "It's an ache, but Jesus, it's so bad. *Fuck*." The pain eased and she caught her breath. Goddamn, was this another joy of pregnancy?

"I've got ibuprofen," Heather said.

"No, thanks." She was only supposed to take Tylenol. For someone who wasn't even sure what she wanted to do about her pregnancy, she'd done her homework. "Damn, I hope that was it."

"PMS fun?"

"Something like that. Whew." She waved a hand to cool her flushed face, then looked back to the task at hand. "When do you get your new car?" she asked Heather. The old one had "shit the bed," as Heather put it, not worth the money to replace the engine. Flynn had found her a used one through a coworker's brother or something.

"Not 'til the weekend, probably. Worth the wait, though—looks like a good little car. Yaris, it's called, which is a stupid-ass name. Sounds like a nickname for your twat. But it's supposed to be reliable. Not a scratch on it, Mike said, which'll be nice after driving that rust bucket for twelve years…"

Laurel nodded, half listening. The pain hadn't gone, merely softened. She felt its nagging pulse and moved in tiny, cautious motions as she worked. There were only three cookies left to ice when another spasm hit, harsh as the first. She moaned and doubled over, staggering to a chair to sit.

"Shit, girl, you okay?"

Laurel shook her head, then nodded, unsure. Goddamn, six weeks pregnant and she was already huffing and puffing her way through the pain—how the heck would *birth* feel, if things went that way?

"Ah, fuck." She squeezed her eyes shut and put her hands to her back, trying to radiate their heat into the spot, praying it would calm again soon. There was more, now—cramps deep in her belly, squeezing sensations shot through with hot shocks of pain.

"I've got Vicodin," Heather said. "It might be expired, but—"

"No, no. Christ, this hurts *so* much."

"You need me to get you to Urgent Care?"

"I don't know. I don't know." It was hard to think, and scary besides.

"I could call a cab— Oh. Laurel."

She opened her eyes, finding Heather's blue ones wide.

"Baby, you're bleeding."

Laurel looked down to discover a maroon patch spreading across the beige chair pad between her thighs. "Oh. Oh my God."

Heather put out a hand, all business. "C'mon. Come to the bathroom. We'll get you sorted out."

Too frightened to argue, Laurel followed in an awkward, tight-legged shuffle, horrified by the wet heat soaking her underwear and jeans.

I'm losing it.

I'm losing it.

Though they were alone in the apartment, Heather shut the bathroom door behind them. "Stand in the tub and get those pants off."

Laurel did, barely aware that she was now naked from the waist down before Flynn's sister. The blood was bright, bright as cherry Kool-Aid. Her back pulsed cruelly but it was her belly she felt now, with terrible clarity. Cramps as though someone were twisting ropes inside her.

Heather handed her one warm, damp hand towel and set a dry one on the tub's edge. "Here, baby. Get yourself cleaned up. I'm gonna find you a pair of pants."

Laurel could only nod and obey. While Heather was gone, she tenderly wiped away the blood, then stood there with the dry towel clenched between her thighs. She could feel it still flowing, see it turning the periwinkle terry cloth the color of merlot.

Heather returned shortly, a lump of patterned fleece tucked under her arm. She unfurled it with a wan smile, revealing a pair of pajama pants covered in hot pink flamingos. "Kim's. Festive, right?"

Laurel mustered the world's limpest smile and looked to the towel.

"How far along?" Heather asked quietly.

She jerked her head back up, feeling ten times more naked than she actually was. "Pardon?"

"I had three miscarriages," Heather said, crouching to root beneath the sink. She set a plastic pack of maxi pads on the closed toilet and stood. "It's no fun, I know."

"You think that's what this is?" Laurel asked, voice a tiny whisper. She didn't have the luxury of googling "six weeks pregnant backache bleeding" just now.

Heather nodded. "Sorry, baby." She'd never addressed Laurel by anything other than her name, now three times in five minutes she'd called her "baby". It was weird. Weird and comforting. "Does Mike know?"

Laurel nodded. "Yeah. It wasn't planned or anything…"

"How's that towel?"

She eased it gingerly from her body, folded it, pressed a clean section to the spot. It came away red, but the gush had eased. "I think it's slowing down."

"Good. I brought you some of Kim's undies. I know that's not your idea of a party but hey, there'll be a pad, right?" As she said it, she stripped the waxed-papery strips off a maxi pad's adhesive and pressed it into the underwear, careful and meticulous as though she were wrapping a present. "You keep the rest—we're a tampon house."

Laurel cracked a tiny, frightened smile at that.

"I can't give you a lift, but I could call you a cab."

"Do you think I need to go to a hospital?" she asked.

Heather shook her head. "I doubt it. Call your doctor's nurse line, if they have one, but this looks pretty textbook, speakin' from experience. If I were you, I'd go home and take it easy."

She nodded. "Yeah, you're probably right. And a cab would be good, thanks." No way she was taking the T, that much was clear.

"You got it. Here." Heather handed her the underwear and set the pajamas on the tub's edge. She picked up the maxi-pad package and studied it, sparing Laurel an audience as she got dressed.

"Like I said, I had three. I'm happy to talk about it, if you ever need to."

"When?" Laurel asked, tugging the fleece up her legs. It felt odd, dry and clean and *cozy*, even as the rest of the world seemed to be falling down around her.

"One was after Kim," Heather said, "when Robbie and I were trying for another kid. Two were before Kim. With those, it was like my body knew what was best for me, since my heart or my religion would never let me get rid of a baby. I prayed for those ones, even if I never came out and spoke the words for real. I felt real guilty both times, like I'd made it happen, but I was relieved. They were a couple years apart, a couple different guys, neither of them up to the challenge—and I wasn't, either. They were blessings. I can say that now." Though she crossed herself as she did.

To Laurel, this didn't feel like a blessing, or an answered prayer. This felt like robbery. Not robbery of a child, necessarily, but the theft of her will, her choice. Flynn's as well.

"I'm not saying that's what this is for you, though," Heather said. "You're different than I was when I was younger. You'll make a great mom, if you go there. It wasn't meant to be, this time, and who can say why."

Who, indeed? And how the hell was she going to tell Flynn?

"Don't say anything to your brother, please."

"Of course not."

"Tell him I had a migraine or something, and that I'm sorry. Let him enjoy the party, and I'll tell him when I'm calmer." And once she'd stopped crying, which she sensed she'd start doing the second she made it to her place, her room. Or maybe just the backseat of the cab.

"Don't worry about Mike. You just worry about yourself. You have a hot water bottle at home?"

"No."

"Borrow ours. It'll help. And that Vicodin's yours, just say the word."

"No, thanks." She stepped out of the tub, feeling no less naked for the borrowed pajamas clashing with her garnet-colored sweater. Garnet. Christ, that color looked so garish now. So cruel.

Heather left for a minute and returned with a tote bag. Inside were the pads, Laurel's jeans in a plastic sack, a hot water bottle, and another bottle—red wine.

She smiled. "Not as good as Vicodin, but it can't hurt."

"Thanks."

"Cab's on its way."

"Cool." So *not* cool in any way imaginable, that any of this was happening. But one thing was certain amid the fear and confusion— she wanted to get away as soon as possible. She didn't want to risk running into Flynn. Didn't want to catch sight of his face, because that'd be the end of her. She wanted to get home, get into her own pajamas, hole up in bed and cry until anything, anything at all, made sense.

CHAPTER SEVEN

Since many miscarriages occur so early that a woman may not even realize that she is pregnant, it can be difficult to estimate how common miscarriage actually is. Some experts believe that as many as half of all fertilized eggs die before implantation—

Thump thump thump.

Laurel jumped at the knock on the bathroom door, halfway to a heart attack.

"Yeah?"

"It's me." Flynn's voice permeated the wood, a rumble that both comforted and unnerved her.

She was sitting on the tile, back against the tub, phone in hand. Neither of her roommates had been in when she'd gotten home, and just as well. She clicked out of the browser app and shut off her phone. "Come in."

The door swung in and there he was. Familiar man in a familiar space, and yet she felt so utterly, irretrievably lost.

He did a double-take, surprised to find her on the floor. "Hey. How's your head?"

She had no reply for that, so she shrugged, no doubt looking sheepish as fuck. "How was the party?"

"Shitty without you. But also pretty special. I brought you a hunk of cake and some Vicodins Heather insisted you might want." He held up a paper grocery bag then set it on the counter. "I didn't explain exactly how terrible an idea that was, obviously."

"She's sweet in her weird way."

"Don't let her hear you say that." He closed the toilet and took a seat. "I didn't know you got migraines. Is it a pregnancy thing?"

"I...I don't think so."

"Wouldn't you rather be someplace dark?"

She tried to smile, tried to be candid and brave and dignified, but one twitch of her lips and her entire face crumpled. Tears streaked her cheeks, burning hot.

"Whoa, honey." He was on his knees in a beat, cupping her shoulders. "What's going on?"

She tried to speak but nothing came, only a rusty squeak. She grabbed the maxi-pad package from the floor beside the toilet, held it up, flung it at the wall with a flash of anger.

His brows drew together, expression darkening from confusion to horror. "Wait. What *is* going on?"

"It's gone." The words felt odd, watery, coming from the roof of her mouth, somehow, not her throat. She gulped air. "The pregnancy. It just... I just started bleeding, at your sister's."

"Like a miscarriage?"

"Yeah. Exactly like that."

For a moment he could only shake his head, looking lost. Looking slapped. "Jesus, Laurel... Does it hurt?"

"Yeah. So bad." The pitiful, ringing truth of that opened something inside her, tears coming fast as though a dam had burst. "It hurts really, *really* bad."

"How?"

"My back. And there's cramps. But mostly it's my back."

"What can I do?"

"Not much."

"Does it… Are you bleeding now?"

"Yeah, loads."

He squeezed her hands. "Fuck me. Heather said you had a headache."

She nodded, catching her breath. She stole one of her hands back to wipe her running nose. "I asked her to tell you that."

His brow knitted. "What?"

"I didn't want to wreck the party for you."

"The fuck?" He paused, caught himself. Sighed and let her other hand go and rubbed his face. He leaned over and freed the toilet paper roll from the dispenser and unfurled a long banner of it to hand to her. "Sorry. I'm not angry at you. I'm just…fuck if I know. Upset, I guess."

"I don't blame you."

Those blue eyes looked so tired. "So this happened *hours* ago? How could you not know how bad I'd want to be with you while you're going through this?"

"I didn't know if I wanted that."

Hurt settled across his face like a shadow.

"Not because you aren't a part of this," she said, and blew her nose. "Not because you don't have a right to know or to care, or to want to help. It's hard to explain." It was that same instinct that urged cats to hide themselves away when they gave birth, wasn't it? The same one that made women so grumpy at the height of PMS. Something primal and isolating.

His expression softened. "What happened? To the baby, I mean."

She wished he wouldn't call it that—it was an embryo. Had been. Nothing more than a little squiggle of cells, or so she took comfort in imagining. She shrugged. "Something genetic, probably."

He seemed to go pale at that.

"It's *really* common. Something like half of pregnancies end in miscarriage. Usually before a woman even knows about it."

"Oh."

"It's nothing either of us did wrong, or anything wrong with our bodies, or anything we could have prevented. This one just decided not to sign the lease."

He smiled grimly, seeming a touch relieved by her levity.

"You're allowed to be sad," she said, and leaned forward to squeeze his arm. The motion triggered a fresh cramp and it took everything she had not to let it show. "Or to feel relieved, or any other thing. This was your experience too, brief as it was."

"I'm here to be whatever you need."

"Same."

He scooted over to sit beside her, curled a palm around the back of her head, scrunched her hair and coaxed her face to his neck. He held her for a long time, rubbing her aching back with a hot, broad palm as she felt the tick of his jugular vein against her lips.

"It really hurts, huh?" he asked softly.

"So much. Like the worst period ever."

"How long does it take to... Fuck, I don't know—"

"About ten days. I called my doctor's office. The bleeding tapers off in time. And there's the cramps and backaches, but those get easier too."

"What can I do for you?"

She shrugged. "Back rubs? Patience? Let me hole up and watch crap TV and be weepy and not take it personally if I need to be alone...?"

He nodded. "I'll try. And how do you *feel?"* he asked again, tone making it plain he wasn't talking about her body.

"I feel a lot of things. Sad, and powerless...but also a little relieved, maybe."

His hand made slow circles across her back.

"I wasn't ready to make that decision, no matter which way I landed on it," she said. "How do *you* feel?"

"Doesn't matter how I feel. Only matters that I be whatever it is you're needing."

"It absolutely *does* matter what you feel. You can tell me." Was he relieved too, and didn't want to make her feel unsupported? Or was he actually *heartbroken*, but didn't want her to think she'd let him down?

Shit, *did* she want to know how he felt about it?

"I don't know what I feel yet," he said.

"Okay."

"Was it because... Did I make this happen?" he asked in a rush of breath.

Her eyes widened and she turned to him. "The miscarriage?"

"The other night, when things got rough..."

"Oh, no. No, no, no. It doesn't work like that. I promise."

He nodded but she could read on his face he wasn't ready to believe her yet.

"Seriously, Flynn, that wasn't anything to do with it. It was just something about the embryo. It wasn't meant to be, so it... I dunno. It just blinked out."

"How big was it?"

"Like a sesame seed, I think."

"So you didn't have to see it, or..." He trailed off.

She shook her head. "Nothing like that."

"Okay. And are you comfortable, sittin' on the floor like this?"

"No, not particularly."

He was on his feet the next moment, offering a hand to help her up.

Laurel stood, her butt cold and achy from sitting on the tile for so long, head swimmy and eyes itchy from the crying. She let him lead her to her bedroom. She crept across the comforter, each movement of her legs twinging something deep inside her. The pad between her legs felt like a diaper. Like a punishment.

Flynn sat across from her, making her bed seem tiny. He'd never spent the night, and they'd only screwed around in her room maybe three times—Laurel was a combination of courteous and shy when it came to having sex within roommates' earshot, and to be fair, a muted Flynn was a complete waste. It just made a million times more sense, fucking at his place.

"You want some tea or something?" he asked. "A drink? You can have booze again, at least."

"No, no drink." It sounded nice, but it felt wrong. Felt too familiar and natural a choice. Too easy. "Thank you."

They were quiet for a long time.

"What are you thinking about?" she finally asked.

"I'm thinking, 'How can this have come to seem so real in next to no time?'"

That stung, but she didn't fault him for it. She'd had the same thought.

"I dunno. But you're right, it did. Even ambivalent as I was, when I realized what was happening, I was so panicky, so frightened for…for *it*. I felt so helpless, like some tiny creature was in crisis and I couldn't do anything to rescue it." And knowing that made her wonder how on earth she'd have felt if she'd chosen to get an abortion, or if she'd have been able to.

"It should've been me there with you, not Heather." His voice didn't break but it sounded odd. Thin, or brittle. Unlike she'd ever heard it.

"You couldn't have known. You were working."

He held his tongue.

"Would you get me some water?" she asked, more to give him a task than anything else.

"Sure. Want any cake?"

"Not just now, thanks."

He came back with the glass and they sat on her bed for a long time, trading quiet words of no particular import. The backaches came and went and he massaged the spot while she hugged the hot water bottle to her crampy middle. In time they wound up spooning, his warm body plastered to her aching muscles, the strength of his arms a small comfort.

"It's weird," she mumbled, breaking long minutes' silence, "but you know what I think upsets me most about this whole thing?"

"What?"

"The way it ended… I'll never know what I would have decided, now."

He sat up, studying her face. "No?"

She shook her head. "I have no idea. I don't know what I would have decided, and I don't know what that decision would have done to us. To you."

"I do," he said.

"Oh?"

"I'd have stayed with you, either way."

"Yeah?"

"No question. And if we didn't have a kid this time, I'd hope we'd have one in two years, or five, or ten, or maybe not at all, if that seemed like the right thing."

"That's really sweet." And actually quite profound. No man had ever told Laurel he wanted her to be the mother of his child before. Not even close. Not even close to close. "You're a refreshingly simple man."

He laughed, a tiny little closed-lip *mm* of a sound.

"What?"

"I'm not that simple."

"I beg to differ."

Flynn shook his head. "If any man ever did to you for real the shit I pretend to, I would *literally* murder him. You think I know what to even make of that?"

"But you know it's different. Different in every way."

"Doesn't mean I don't doubt it now and then. Doubt who the fuck I even am, wonder exactly how thin a scrap of conscience separates me and the sickest fuckers walkin' this earth."

Now Laurel shook her head, smiling. "Don't doubt yourself for a second. I don't."

"God knows what I did to deserve you."

"Plenty."

He opened his mouth. Shut it. He regarded her for a long moment, then got to his feet with a grunt. "Hang on a minute. Need somethin' from my car."

"Okay."

That lie about having a headache was absolutely true now, Laurel noted, her brain feeling pickled. She headed to the bathroom, washed her face and brushed her teeth and changed her pad, feeling tender more in her heart than her sex. Back in her bedroom, she propped the reheated hot water bottle against a pillow and sat with her lower back pressed to it, hugging her knees.

Flynn returned with his jacket slung over his arm. "You lied to me earlier, having Heather tell me you had a migraine."

"I know. I'm—"

"I lied to you too." He sat at the edge of her bed, his hip touching her toes.

"You did?"

He looked down at his jacket, now folded in his lap. "Don't think I've ever lied to you before. Can't think why I would have."

Indeed. A man as blunt and unapologetic as Flynn had no reason to. Her curiosity was thoroughly piqued, stomach just a little queasy. "What was the lie?"

"I didn't work today. There was no overtime shift."

"Oh. Okay."

"I had an errand to run." He unfolded his jacket and slipped his hand inside a pocket. When he slid it out, he was holding a small, polished wood box, opening it before Laurel's imagination got a chance to jump to wild conclusions. Even if it had, it could never have predicted the ring she was suddenly staring at.

"I know I bought this after I found out you were pregnant—"

"Oh my God."

"—but what's happened doesn't change how I feel, or what I want. Thinkin' we were gonna go through whatever we were together, raising a kid, or goin' through whatever the fuck sort of head-trip an abortion must be… It just felt obvious. It just felt right, like, this woman's got the power to change my life in massive, mind-blowing ways, and I knew no matter what you decided, I only wanted to be next to you. So I'm hopin' you'll say you wanna be next to me, for whatever's gonna come next."

"Jesus, Flynn." Her head was swimming. What she really wanted was to touch the ring, to see it up close, but she didn't dare. It didn't feel right. It didn't feel wrong, either, just… Not yet. Just not now.

When she didn't reach for it, he turned the little box around and regarded it a moment. "Do you think it's pretty?"

"I think it's gorgeous."

"Anne told me you would."

She had to laugh, floored to think there'd been such a conspiracy afoot. "You lied about your whereabouts so you could sneak off with another woman behind my back? While I slaved away, icing cookies for your niece's—"

"You want to try it on?"

"I— No. Not yet."

A pause. "Is that a no, no?"

"It's not a no. It's a... I'm not sure. It's a... It's an ask-me-again, when I'm not hurting so bad. Ask me when I can wrap my head around it."

"Ten days, you said?"

She smiled. "In a month, or six months. I know you're not doing this out of pity, or to try to cheer me up or distract me, but... Shit, I feel like I'm messing this up. But ask me again later." Her heart was too banged up right now to muster the giddy flutterings such a moment deserved.

"Did I completely wreck this?" he asked.

"No. Not at all. You're amazing. Pretend I'm as blunt and transparent as you, Flynn, and just take me at my word on this one. Ask me again when things have gotten back to normal and it feels like the right time to you."

He snapped the box shut and tucked it in his jacket with a little smirk. "When my mind's made up, it's made up, so it can only feel right."

She smirked back. "Very smooth. I wish I had an answer now, trust me. But what happened today... I spend a lot of time trying not to feel things. To hide or to get numb or ignore my issues. But this... I think I need to *feel* this, what I'm going through now. All of it. This isn't the sort of pain I want to pack up and stuff down and ignore and have to deal with later. I just want to feel the ugly fuck out of it until I'm okay again. Get it all over with."

He nodded.

"When I'm done doing that, your question deserves my full attention. My full, sober, rational attention."

"I hear you."

She sighed, tired but calm, finally. "I'm not going to be much fun for the next couple weeks."

"I'm not with you because it's easy, honey."

She looked up, struck twice by that remark—first by its sweetness, but then by a tiny backhand, the implication that she was difficult. But she closed her mouth on a protest, because it was true and she knew it, and furthermore she knew it wasn't a criticism. Merely a fact.

"Why *are* you with me?" she asked, careful to sound curious and not defensive.

His answer came at once. "The way you make me feel."

"How do I make you feel?"

"Lots of ways. You make me feel understood, I guess. And appreciated, and useful. And trusted. And out-of-my-mind horny beyond belief."

She laughed. "Good answer."

"I feel like you get me. Whatever it is I offer, it's something you want, or need. And if it isn't always easy to be with you, when you're depressed or whatever, I know I'm not easy to be with all the time either. I know sometimes I'm kind of a dick, and I know being with me, sexually, takes you way outside your comfort zone."

"That's really not so much of a sacrifice," she said, blushing faintly.

"But it's intense, and it takes effort. I appreciate it."

"It's not a favor," she added.

"Neither's taking care of you when you're having a hard time."

Tears welled and slipped free, tracing hot paths down her cheeks. "Thanks. It's nice to hear you put it that way."

"And takin' care of you right now, this ain't easy, either. But it's not a favor. It's not even a duty. It's just what we do for each other."

She nodded. Still, she wished her higher-maintenance aspects involved filthy, kinky sex instead of mental health crises.

They fell silent, and Laurel seemed to leave her body for a minute, as though her mind took a step back, hovering just outside her skin. She saw the two of them eight months into a romance, struck by how this looked nothing like any theoretical locket portrait she might have been carrying around, depicting the future love of her life. Physically, this man was more than she'd ever have paired herself with; more aggressively, blatantly masculine than she'd realized she was into. But it went far beyond that.

"This isn't how I imagined it would look, being in love," she said slowly, teasing the idea free, like an archaeologist brushing the dust from a bone. "Like, in *actual* love, not just the kind you feel at the start."

"How do you mean?"

"Just this, right now... When you see people in love in movies or wherever, it's all good feelings. Grand gestures and proclamations and kissing in the rain. I never thought it could feel this intimate, something as painful as this. Something this visceral, and ugly, and sad. But I don't know if I've ever felt this close to anyone."

His smile was small, somehow fragile.

"I mean, I never imagined I'd let a guy have sex with me during my period. But this is like... I dunno. I guess what I'm saying is, it amazes me how unafraid of the female body you are."

"Helpful when you're a straight guy."

"No, you have no idea how terrified guys are of women's bodily functions. And how gross it makes us feel. But you really don't give a shit. Are you *sure* you were raised Catholic?"

He laughed. "When you're into what I am... It takes communication. Plus I attract pretty ballsy, outspoken women."

Laurel nodded. She had a meek streak, but she *had* gone after him, at the start. That was Flynn's m.o. He didn't do the pursuing, at least not until a woman knew what she was in for. And Laurel supposed that, yes, it did take a certain shameless type of gal to chase a man as intimidating as Flynn. It gave her a funny little jolt of pride and surprise to realize she was one of them.

"If a woman's too shy to acknowledge the existence of her period, she's probably not up for negotiating a rape scene," he said.

"I suppose not. And really, I'd happily trade mystique and discretion for honesty. And to be with a man who'll go out in a snowstorm and get me tampons."

"It wasn't a storm."

"And potato chips."

He shrugged. "You keep tendin' my wounds, I'll keep you in snacks and lady-plugs."

"It's a deal." She laughed, caught by a thought. "Could those be our vows?"

He looked up, gaze soft but loaded. In time, he smiled. "I think we can do better than that."

"I don't suppose I could look at the ring again?"

"Sure."

Her breath caught as he dug through the folds of his jacket and produced the little box. She'd been so floored when he'd first whipped it out, she'd really only registered the barest details—*diamond, sparkly, proposal.*

He passed her the box and she opened it, its tiny hinge silent. The ring was seated in a bed of dove-gray velvet, almost as though the diamond were floating there. "Wow." It was big. Not garish, but larger than she'd ever have set her heart on. "Not to be tacky, but is this real?"

"Yeah."

"Wow," she said again, and he chuckled. "I like the shape." Not a circle—a softly rounded rectangle.

"It's a cushion cut," he announced with an overdone know-it-all air.

"The jeweler tell you that?"

"Yup."

"It's beautiful. Like, *beautiful*." She slid it out. The band was simple and slender, nicely balanced with the size of the stone. She turned it this way and that, watching the lamplight dance in the facets, feeling woozy to imagine she could wear this. All she had to do was say the word.

Not yet. Not until there was enough room inside her for all the joy that moment deserved to inspire. She slipped the ring back into its little slot, sad to shut it away in the dark.

"How'd you know my size? Anne?"

He nodded. "She snuck in and stole one of your rings."

"Which one?"

"Silver, with a blue stone in it."

She smiled. "Clever little sneak."

"I didn't tell her about the pregnancy," he said.

"I wouldn't have imagined you would."

"You gonna tell her?"

She nodded. "Yeah, I will. She knows me too well not to notice I'm having a hard time."

"You call in sick to work, I hope?"

"I have tomorrow off, so I'll play it by ear. The distraction might be welcome."

"You said you want to feel it all."

"I do. But I don't want to wallow in it, either. I just want to make sure I don't half-ass this…this mourning, or whatever this is. I don't want to white-knuckle my way through it, keeping manically busy, or cover over it with alcohol, or try to sleep through it. It deserves to be felt." She paused, feeling like some hippy-dippy weirdo.

"Whatever you need. I'll keep this fucker safe until you're ready to make its acquaintance," he said, flashing the box then burying it back inside his coat pocket.

"Deal."

She studied him for a long time. He looked different. Perhaps it was the comparably girly setting, atop her full mattress as opposed to his king, on her turquoise comforter, in a room with regular-sized windows and a normal-height ceiling. He looked new. Handsome in a softer way than usual.

He was an attractive man, she thought, but not everyone's cup of tea. He didn't have a charming smile—more a cocky smirk—and his hands were rough, same as his accent and his words and his kinks. Many women would prefer a polished type, dazzling and pedigreed as that diamond, or perhaps one as smooth and dignified as onyx. Flynn was brick, blunt and abrasive and honest, with hard edges and common good looks as plain as his speech. His body was ridiculous, though. It was a nice balance. A model-handsome face capping a physique like his would look like a caricature.

For the briefest moment, she wondered what it might have looked like. Their child.

If he gets his way, I've got all the time in the world to find out.

"You want to be alone?" he asked, perhaps mistaking her silence for distance.

She shook her head. "No. I want you here."

"Good."

"I want you to spend the night, if you want that too."

"I wanna be whatever you need."

"You always are." And what she needed right now was a strong pair of arms holding her, keeping her together even as the ground seemed to be crumbling away beneath her feet.

CHAPTER EIGHT

"SOMETHING TO DRINK WHILE YOU WAIT?"

"Water's fine." Flynn looked past the waitress to the restaurant's front windows. He thought to tack on a tardy "Thanks" just as she turned to walk away. His etiquette was rusty, and his mood wasn't helping.

The place wasn't fancy, just a little Sicilian hole-in-the-wall at the edge of the North End. The food was phenomenal—he'd been here before with Laurel—but the napkins were paper and most of the entrées were less than twenty bucks. Still, if he wasn't ordering off a board tacked above a row of registers, it felt strange.

He checked his phone. Five after. Not like Laurel to be late, but also not like Laurel to spring a last-minute date on him. They hardly ever went on dates, probably only once or twice a month. They'd been on precisely zero the past few weeks, and if he was honest, he wasn't really in the mood. But Laurel had sounded so excited over the phone, there was no way he could've said no.

The period following the miscarriage had been rough. He'd done his best to be whatever she needed, but as often as not, she hadn't seemed sure of what that was. She'd been clingy one moment, cool the next, acting as though she'd rather be away from him but denying that she did. Even when he'd seemed to be doing exactly what she needed, he'd felt lost.

She'd caught him just as he'd been leaving work today, wanting him to meet her at six. He'd been hoping to go to the gym instead, but he'd dutifully gone home and showered off the plaster dust and dressed in his least beat-up jeans and the black sweater she'd given him for Christmas, ran a cloth over his only dress shoes. Glancing around, he figured he passed, even if he felt like a rhino perched on this spindly wooden chair. Even if he was the only patron with stitches bisecting their left eyebrow. Or any other body part, come to that.

Oh fucking well.

He'd give just about anything to be back in Southie, beating the shit out of a heavy bag, feeling nothing. But if the price was letting Laurel down, he wasn't willing to pay it.

It was mid-March, and a springy March at that. Only a few scabs of brown snow still clung to the shadier sidewalks, and the air smelled good, like winter was officially in the rearview. The sky was blue beyond the restaurant's tall windows; the days were getting longer.

Laurel was getting stronger. Seeming more like her old self.

Flynn wished he could say the same.

I know this feeling. I've lived through it before.

It was grief. No mistaking it. But grief this real and this nagging, for a near-microscopic little—

A tap on his shoulder turned Flynn's head, and there she was. Smiling, looking gorgeous. Looking *happy*, her red hair pulled back in a ponytail and a few inches of bare leg visible between the tops of her fancy boots and the hem of a wool skirt. Her coat was folded over her arm.

"Hey, beautiful." He stood and kissed her cheek, pulled out the opposite chair for her.

"Hey. Thanks." She draped her coat over the chair back and sat, letting him go through that weird charade of pretending like he was helping as she scooted her seat in.

"Didn't see you come in," he said, sitting.

"There's two doors. Sorry I'm late."

"Barely."

"You look quite sexy," she said, bobbing her eyebrows. "Nice sweater."

He mustered a smile, feeling like a fraud. "Thanks. My old lady got it for me."

"Not *so* old." She pulled a menu over.

"You look hot as fuck," he told her. Her legs drove him up a wall. Always had. He wished she wore skirts more often. It was nice to catch himself thinking it, too. The past couple weeks hadn't exactly been erotic.

The miscarriage was one thing of course. Pain, both physical and emotional, had consumed her, and being the strong one had consumed him in return. Even now, with the physical business of it done and Laurel seeming all but normal, he wasn't ready for sex yet, himself. She might like to go on about his lack of squeamishness when it came to the female body, but he was intimidated by the whole prospect. Not grossed out, just...worried. Worried he might hurt her. Worried she'd cry. Worried he'd fuck it all up, and on the other end worried they'd never get back there, never be the same again.

But something about the skirt and the boots gave him the thinnest sliver of hope.

"Why the getup?" he asked.

"I have my reasons." She was wearing makeup, too. Mascara, and the stuff you put on the lids that Flynn could never remember the name of. "I've worn nothing but jeans and pajamas and my work clothes for two weeks," she said. "I guess I got sick of looking at myself."

"Well, you look awesome."

She blushed, visibly, even in the low light. "You too."

The waitress arrived with two glasses of ice water and greeted Laurel. "A drink for you?"

Laurel scrambled for the wine list. "Oh, let's see... Whatever you'd recommend that's red and dry and less than eight bucks a glass...?"

"Ignore the bit about the price," Flynn cut in.

"I can personally vouch for either the Syrah or the Round Pond cabernet," the waitress offered.

"Syrah, please."

"Do you two need a few more minutes with the menus?"

"Yes, thanks. No rush." Laurel flashed a big smile. For obvious reasons, she was exceedingly nice to wait staff and always bullied Flynn into tipping way more than he normally would.

Once the waitress was gone, he said, "Haven't seen you drink in ages."

"Yeah, I haven't. Not since before the test. I wanted to make sure I wasn't self-medicating, but since I feel pretty good today, I figure why not?"

Lucky you. He caught himself, shamed by the petty thought. "Good for you."

"How was work?" She was just a little off, he noticed. Nervous? Guilty?

"Same old shit," he said. "Minus the usual workout. Tell me about your day."

Oh, there it was—that smile. Definitely nervous. "It was...good."

"You look like you got somethin' to share. Spill it."

She bit her lip, pink cheek going round, making his belly all warm. "Well, I applied for two more jobs."

"Nice. Where?"

"Both on the T, or close to it. One's downtown, the other's in Malden. That makes seven I've applied for this week."

"Fuckin' fantastic. You interested in either of them?"

She shrugged. "Enough. Anything in my field is what I'm after. No more being picky," she said, sitting up straight. "I used that as an excuse for way too long."

"Well, good job."

"Thanks." She was doing it again, looking all cagey.

"What?"

She leaned in, the end of her ponytail brushing the table. "I got invited to interview."

He blinked. "You did?"

She nodded, any cool act she'd been mustering gone in an instant. "I did."

"Where?"

"A place I applied to last week. It's a biotech company in Kendall Square—there's an opening for an entry-level mechanical engineer, and the salary's pretty great. I mean, not that I'll get it necessarily, though I did do my degree project on the same sorts of systems they specialize in…"

He let her go on, not taking in much of the specifics but getting swept up in how excited she sounded, how hopeful and hyper and awake. Nice to get pulled out of his own gloom for a couple minutes.

Her wine arrived just as she seemed to be winding down. She raised the glass with a cheesy-ass, expectant smile.

Flynn lifted his water and they toasted. "That's fucking phenomenal, honey. Well done."

"Thanks."

"Dinner was already on me, but now we're both required to get dessert."

"Dinner ought to be on me," she said, voice turning soft and private. "I know I haven't been the easiest person to be around lately—"

"Hush. When's the interview?"

"Friday. Hence the skirt. I needed to make sure I had an outfit worth turning up in."

"They're not wastin' any time. You must be a catch."

"Or they must be desperate."

He shot her a stern look. "Knock that shit off. They'd be lucky to have you. Just make sure your boss is a fugly old fucker, that's all I ask."

She laughed. "I'll be sure to ask about that during the interview."

"Wish you'd told me over the phone. I'd have found you some flowers."

"Save them for when I actually get a job."

"I know just the kind. The stinky white-and-pink ones."

She rolled her eyes, smiling. "Oriental lilies." Her favorites.

"That's what I said."

"You know what you're ordering?"

"No clue."

"Me neither." She handed him a menu. "Let's focus, shall we?"

He scanned the options, not taking much in.

She's moving on. And so she should. Moving on from the grief and confusion and pain, and it seemed liked she'd dodged a bout of deeper depression to boot. But as she moved on, Flynn felt as if he was still stuck at square one, shell-shocked and helpless.

Suck it up, asshole. This whole situation… It had been her decision from the very start, her body that would've assumed the work of a pregnancy if she'd decided to keep it, and in the end, her body that bore the torture of the miscarriage. He got no say, and that was how it should be.

Though he couldn't help but feel like the last man at the wake, alone with the casket while his ride home pulled away from the curb and left him behind.

CHAPTER NINE

LAUREL DOUBTED she'd ever eaten a meal half as delicious as tonight's. The secret ingredient was relief, she supposed—relief that her body wasn't hurting anymore, that she was finally free of maxi pads and backaches and that nagging feeling of tenderness, more emotional than physical.

She'd gone to see her gyno a few days earlier, to make sure the miscarriage had run its course. Everything had looked good, considering, and while she'd been there they'd inserted an IUD, as she no longer trusted the Pill any farther than she could spit one. As a bonus, the IUD didn't rely on hormones, which was bound to be better for her moods.

Mixed with the relief was excitement. *I have an interview.* Something about the miscarriage—or the scary, brief reality of the pregnancy— had lit a fire under her ass. She'd applied for more jobs in the past two weeks than she bet she had in the six months preceding them. This was the first interview she'd been offered in all that time. She wasn't foolish enough to get her hopes up, but just scoring an invitation felt big.

She looked to the driver's seat, at Flynn's stoic face lit by the dash and the chasing streetlights, gaze nailed to the road. Fists at ten and two. Which was a little odd, as half the time he drove one-handed. He seemed strained, in fact. She'd been so wrapped up in her good news, she'd failed to notice until now.

"You missing your workout?" she asked.

"No way I was passing up a date with you. Especially not with something to celebrate." Pretty words, but his tone was strange and flat and *off*, like an instrument missing a string.

She nearly asked if he was okay, but held her tongue. She was guarded, she knew that, as guarded as Flynn was normally forthcoming. She'd never known him to hold back, and she was at a loss for how to approach him.

You're overthinking it. Approach it the Michael Flynn way. "You all right?"

"Yeah. Yeah, just tired."

Liar. "I'm only going to ask this one more time—are you sure?"

He looked her way. "I'm sure."

"Okay."

His eyes sought the road. "You know how I get when I don't blow off steam after work. That's all."

"Oh, sorry. Is it too late to—"

"I'm fine." He said it too quick, too gruff.

Laurel watched the scene streaking by her window—brick and ocean and sleeping steel cranes and more brick—for the rest of the drive, triumph forgotten, worries settling in like old friends around a smoky bar.

It's been over two weeks since we've had sex. That couldn't be helping his anxiety. Still, the thought buoyed her some; she felt strong again, stronger than before the pregnancy, even. No doubt he was waiting for her to initiate, after what she'd been through. Well, no problem there. She'd be happy to peel the sweater off him when they got back to his place, remind herself that his body was for more than merely holding her, those hands capable of feats far less kindly than marathon back rubs.

He parked behind his building and they slammed their doors in the quiet night, the rest of South Boston feeling as though it had gone to bed, though it was barely eight.

How much am I up for, tonight?

Probably not role-playing. She didn't want to go there until she felt him return to her, his usual self.

His usual self. It occurred to her then, Flynn was the most consistent person she'd ever known. He didn't have mood swings, not unless bloodlust and horniness counted. He got annoyed now and then, but he never went quiet like this. She supposed most people did, and of course he was entitled to, but something about it… It was unnerving. It felt as though he were made of stone as they rode the elevator up to the fifth floor. Cold and silent.

He let them into the apartment and eased up the lights. Laurel had brought her overnight bag and she tossed it on the loveseat. Force of habit from these past couple of mopey weeks urged her to pull out her pajamas and get comfy, but she caught herself. Not tonight. She was wearing a skirt, after all. It'd be a shame not to get fucked in it.

Flynn was unlacing his shoes at the couch and she passed by on her way to the bathroom, leaned down and planted a kiss on his temple. He kept his eyes on the task. That taste of coolness dug the worry hole deeper, but she forced it from her mind as she brushed her teeth and her hair, dabbed her shiny forehead with a wad of toilet paper.

She looked how she felt—lit up and alive. Maybe a little nervous and rusty, but more awake than she had in so, so long. She'd show

Flynn that she was better again. Show the both of them that her body wasn't a fragile, fractured shell in need of kid gloves.

The red towel was folded on the shelf above the toilet. She eyed it. *No, no goring. Not tonight, anyhow.* She flipped off the light and fan.

He was still on the couch when she exited, perusing a piece of mail, its ripped envelope in one hand.

"Riveting news?" she asked.

"Mm?"

She plopped down beside him. "Your mail. Anything thrilling?"

"Nah. Gas bill."

"At least those'll be getting smaller, now."

"Mm."

He hadn't looked at her once since they'd gotten in, had he? In a blink, she realized what must be going on—he was feeling insecure. What Flynn himself called "Uptown Girl Syndrome." How working-class guys could be real dicks if they were involved with women who outpaced them, education- or profession-wise. Plus Flynn had told her before he'd wanted to be more than a construction worker, once upon a time. He'd wanted to do what she'd trained to, basically, to be a civil engineer or an architect. Maybe her good news, her chance at a career, was giving him blue-collar angst.

She knew better than to ask. If that was the culprit, best to go with carnal distraction, rather than make a big deal of it.

"May I?" she asked, plucking the bill from one of his hands, the envelope from the other. She set them on the coffee table and leaned close, rubbing his chest.

He accepted a kiss—at first stiffly, but softening in seconds, rewarding her with a hot sweep of his tongue. She felt her body soften in reply, relief morphing to excitement. Much as she'd needed to keep herself protected since the miscarriage, kissing this way instantly felt right, felt essential. She'd missed their sexual bond more than she'd realized.

She pulled away, pushed him until he sat back. "Stay there."

"Stay?"

She smiled, feeling wicked and electric, so ready for this. "You'll see."

Hesitance tempered his expression but she was only too happy to show him how solid she felt in her body and her heart. She moved to the floor, twisted around to push the coffee table farther away, then settled between his legs. The familiar bite of grit and hardwood met her bare knees, a welcome reminder of a hundred filthy memories. Memories of what they'd lost track of these past couple weeks.

She splayed her palms over his legs, stroking from his knees to his hips and back down.

"You don't need to…" He trailed off as his lids grew heavy, stare glazing. She warmed through to watch it.

"Of course I don't. I want to." She raked her nails over his hard thighs, loving the shudder that rolled through the length of his body. She went for his belt, slipping the end free of the post, pausing to rub her palm across the shape of his growing erection. He covered her hand with his, wanting to slow it or to follow its motions. She squeezed gently, earning another shiver and a tensing of that hand.

"Honey."

She took that as approval, smiling to herself and turning her attention to the button of his fly.

"Don't," he said softly.

"Why not?" She murmured it, more seduction than question. *I'm not as delicate as you think.*

"Not yet."

"I've missed this," she told him, letting another slow stroke of his straining cock underscore that truth. And if she'd missed this, Flynn had no doubt *mourned* it.

His voice was thick, unsteady. "You don't need to," he said again. He held her hand but she slipped free, seeking his zipper.

"Like I said, I want to." She hurt for it, physically. Literally. Arousal was a hot, grasping ache inside her, and her salivary glands stung and watered, anticipating the weight of his hands on her, guiding her, holding her hair. His voice, mean and bossy once more, a change so welcome after weeks of patient encouragement. She spread his fly open, greeted by that intoxicating scent. It seemed nearly new after all this time.

"Honey, don't."

She cupped him, traced the edge of his erection with her thumb, but then his hand was around her wrist, tight, jerking her away.

"Jesus, Laurel. Knock it off."

She sat back, feeling slapped. She had no words, but her expression seemed to speak for her—he looked chastised in an instant. He scrubbed his hands over his face and hair, eyes squeezed shut, mouth set.

"Sorry," he muttered, not sounding especially sorry.

"*I'm* sorry. I thought you'd be more than up for that, after all this time."

"Not yet."

"Sorry," she said again. "It's just… I'm ready. You've been, like, superhumanly patient, and I wanted to get there again, tonight. I'm ready, really."

In a breath he was up and walking away, zipping up and buckling his belt as he went.

Frozen there on her knees, Laurel could only watch him stride to the sink and fill a glass with water. The hard floor beneath her, so welcome only moments before, felt humiliating. Her throat was tight, words too thick, lodged deep. She managed to pry free the only one that counted right now.

"Flynn?"

He set the glass down and braced both hands on the counter. When he dropped his head she could see his back expand and contract, his breaths looking slow and forced.

"Baby," she said, instantly realizing she'd never called him such a thing before. "I need you to talk to me. Or to tell me to go, and we can talk some other time." Her voice was calm but her heart was pounding. He'd never been like this with her. If he sent her away with no explanation, she'd be a wreck until she heard from him again.

An almighty inhalation swelled his entire frame, then he raised his head. He turned, met her eyes, leaned back against the counter looking older, somehow. After a moment he seemed to wilt, expression going from stony to weary. "Get off the floor, for fuck's sake."

She moved to sit on the coffee table. "Did I say something wrong?"

Another gigantic breath and he rubbed at his face again. "No. Yes and no."

"Tell me."

He dropped his arms and met her stare. "You said you're ready."

She nodded. "I am."

"Well, I'm not."

"Okay. That's fine. I didn't mean to rush you. I just assumed you must be pretty hard up by now." She cracked a little smile, not earning one in return. "You want to talk about it?"

"Not really."

She felt herself tipping from panic into exasperation, her backbone restacking itself. "Well, tell me what's wrong or tell me to go." She brushed the grit from her knees. "It feels like I'm only going to keep saying the wrong thing if you don't help me out, here. Do you want me to go?"

"Yes," he said, his tone soft and cold.

Another psychic slap, and she rose on unsteady legs.

"Wait—no. Sit. Fucking sit."

She did, watching as he made his way across the room. He didn't sit beside her but instead on the floor, his back against the couch and his arms crossed atop his knees. It made him look small, a feat she'd have thought impossible before this moment.

"I'm sorry," he murmured, addressing his wrists or maybe her shins. "I know I'm being a royal dick. I'm just... I'm feelin' a load of stuff and I don't know what the fuck to do with it."

"Tell me."

"I don't want to. You're just gettin' over everything. You deserve to be gettin' over everything. I don't wanna shit all over that."

"'Everything' meaning the miscarriage?"

"Yeah."

"God knows how much time you've spent listening to me cry and talk about it. You're allowed to have feelings about it too."

"No, I'm not."

"Yeah, you *really* are."

He shook his head. "I'm not the one who had to go through that. Not all the pain, in my body, and not all the emotional stuff either. And I was never the one who was stuck havin' to make the decision, beforehand. You've been through plenty. Last thing I want is to drag you back into it when you finally seem happy."

"Well, too bad. It was your experience as much as it was mine. Just because it was my body doesn't mean you don't get to have feelings about it."

A giant, silent sigh seemed to say, *That's your opinion.*

She paused, eyeing the counter. The bottle of wine he'd bought her when he'd picked up the pregnancy test was still there beside the toaster, untouched. She crossed the room and dug through the junk drawer for the opener. She took two of Flynn's hideous Christmas-patterned wine glasses from the cupboard and filled each near to the brim.

His brows rose when she turned, a dose in each hand. She delivered his and took her seat on the table once more.

"I don't drink," he said.

"You're not an alcoholic, though. Just trust me. It might knock some of your feelings loose. Like an emotional laxative for constipated tough guys." She sipped her own wine, enjoying the tight smirk that quirked his lips.

"Booze turns me into an asshole."

"You're already being an asshole. Double down. Let it all out."

He shook his head, but ultimately put the glass to his lips. A deep swallow screwed his face up in a wince. "Jesus. Why d'you let me pick out wine?"

She took another taste, considering. "This is one of your better selections."

"Tastes like cherry rubbing alcohol."

"You're just out of practice. Now choke it down and spill your guts."

She realized in that instant that she was Flynn, tonight. He wasn't necessarily being Laurel, but she was the take-no-bullshit partner, the strong one bullying the lost one into action. It felt nice. She felt...taller.

He suffered through another gulp then set the glass on the floor beside him. He met her gaze. "I dunno what to say."

"Just tell me what you're feeling. Tell me why you pushed me away, when I tried to start something."

"Like I said, I'm not ready."

"Not ready because...?"

"Because...fuck. Because I'm still fuckin' sad, okay?"

"About the miscarriage?"

"Yeah."

"Oh. I'm sorry. I didn't realize." She'd had no clue, in fact. He'd so thoroughly put her feelings first these past couple weeks, she'd come to assume he was doing fine with it all. "I wish I'd known."

"Why? So you could feel even shittier than you already were?" The exhaustion in his voice left the sarcasm toothless.

"Ever since I found out I was pregnant, it's felt like… Like you don't think you get to have any opinions about any of it. Which I *never* agreed with."

He took a deep breath, attention on the hands flexing restlessly between his knees. "I know."

"But you clearly *do* have opinions, and you obviously need to vent them. So tell me about them. You feel sad about the miscarriage. How come?"

He finally met her eyes. "Isn't it obvious?"

She supposed that, yes, it was. "You were hoping I'd keep it?"

He didn't reply immediately, looking hesitant, lost. "Maybe. Maybe I was."

Laurel moved, settling at his side with her glass. Sometimes it was easier to talk about heavy things when eye contact was off the table.

She told the far wall, "You were always allowed to want that." A fresh chill settled over her, nothing to do with the cold floor beneath her butt. *If I'd decided to end it, would you have resented me? Left me over it, in time?* "I wish you'd told me. But I know why you didn't."

"Thing is, nothin' about having a kid right now made any sense. It didn't make sense for you, job-wise. It didn't make sense for us, together, not this soon."

"No."

"It didn't even make sense for me," he said. "I mean, it's not like I've been sittin' around twiddlin' my thumbs, wishin' I was a father. Not at all. I see people around town with strollers lookin' like they haven't slept in a year and I think, 'Thank fuck that's not me, yet.'

And now that it's gone, it's not like I want us to try and get you pregnant all over again."

"But…?"

He shrugged, the black of his sweater rising and slumping in her periphery. "My head was with you, with whatever you decided. But some other part of me…I dunno. It charged me up, imagining it. Or just knowin' about it, knowin' that was going on inside your body. I won't lie, it felt really fucking profound."

"I wish I'd known."

"It might've changed what you decided. And I didn't want that, not when it was just some feeling."

"Feelings are important. More important than logic, sometimes. And it kind of scares me that I didn't know how you felt. Like, if I'd decided to end it, what would you have thought of me? It's my body but it's your life as much as mine that would've been turned upside-down."

"It was always your decision. The stakes were ten times higher for you."

At a loss, she took a sip of wine and Flynn did the same.

"You know what I think bothers me the most?" he asked at length, setting his glass between his feet.

"What?"

"It's how mismatched this feels. Like, how can I be so sure about us—ready to marry you, ready to raise a kid, with or without you—and you have no fucking idea what you want?"

She thought about that long and hard, emotions bubbling up to leave her face hot and no doubt red. "Because one of us knows themselves, and the other's a *fucking* mess." Her voice broke on the swear, and in a blink tears were stinging. She willed them away, not wanting to cry. Not wanting to seem weak, to give this man any reason to pull his punches when it had taken so much pushing to get him to be honest in the first place. Still, fear was rising inside her, gathering dark and dense as a storm cloud. *Where's this going?*

He didn't reply right away.

She'd never felt this cut off from him before, and it couldn't be a coincidence that they hadn't had sex in two weeks. Was that how it worked? Take the fucking away and they just fell to pieces? Was sex that powerful, or was what connected them simply that tenuous, when you got right down to it?

"Look at us," he said quietly. "You're ready to move on, and good for you. But me, I'm stuck feeling all this grief and shit, like the miscarriage started this morning. How can we be so fucking far apart?"

How indeed, when he was close enough for her to feel the heat coming off his body?

"I don't know. Maybe because I've had the luxury of focusing on how I feel this entire time, and you're only now just letting yourself think about it. Or because part of me was relieved by what happened, and you clearly weren't."

"Maybe."

"I hope you know how much I appreciate you being there for me, through all this."

"You told me every single day."

"Good. It's meant a lot. I don't know how I would've survived it all, without you." A couple days into the ordeal she'd told Anne what she was going through, and her friend had been great—eager to console and distract—but it had been Flynn's strong and steady presence that had seen her to the light at the far end of the tunnel. "I only wish I'd known you were hurting this much, so I could've been there for you. We could've hurt together."

"Maybe," he said again.

"Maybe we're not so far apart, after all." She sought his gaze, nervous, desperate for some taste of connection, for proof their bond was still intact. "I feel like I let you down."

He looked to the glass resting between his ankles, shook his head. "You didn't know. I didn't want you to."

"Well, tell me what you need now."

He raised his chin, attention somewhere in the middle distance. "Fuck if I know."

"Time, probably. But anything else you think of, tell me." If only his needs were as obvious as back rubs and ibuprofen.

"Do you want me to go?" she asked.

His lips twitched.

"It's okay if you do. If you're grieving, sometimes that's easiest to do alone."

He picked up his glass from between his feet, draining it then setting it on the table. He turned to face her and she did the same, surprised but relieved when he reached out to cup her neck. He urged her close and kissed her deeply, tasting as he never had in all the time she'd known him. Feeling as he never had either, his lust—if it could be called lust—tinged with something brittle and needy.

She couldn't guess where he wanted this to end up, but she was prepared to find out, to go with him wherever he needed to be.

He grabbed at her hips and she took the cue, straddling his lap. Her skirt rode up, bare legs hugging his clothed ones. Hungry, coarse hands rubbed her thighs, thumbs tracing the hems of her panties at her hips then slipping beneath them.

His kiss matched the touch, feeling more like the Flynn she knew—masterful, if not entirely present. He tugged her close, her soft sex pressing along the seam of his fly and the hard flesh it hid. She nearly asked if he was ready, then caught herself. The time for assurances had passed. Perhaps action was best. Perhaps getting lost in the physical could help them find their way back to each other.

"You feel good," she whispered against his lips. And he did. Rough and eager, and above all, controlled. The hands guiding her hips felt strong, showing her what he wanted. She gave it, rubbing their bodies together, her breasts brushing his chest, mouths losing grace until they broke apart completely. She pressed her lips to the spot where his jaw met his ear, let him hear how ragged her exhalations had grown.

"You want me?" he demanded, voice rumbling through both of their bodies and lighting her on fire.

"So bad."

"What've you missed most?" His tone was a touch cold, a touch callous, but she welcomed it all the same.

"You, being bossy."

He ground her hard against him. "What else?"

"Your cock."

He didn't reply except to suck a long, guttural breath and bury his face against her throat.

Come back to me. She wanted all of him, but she'd take his sexual side only, if that was what was on offer. She'd take whatever iteration of her lover this was, let this sex be his solace or distraction, or her punishment.

Whatever he needed. Whoever he needed to be.

CHAPTER TEN

"WHAT WERE YOU AFTER, BEFORE?" Flynn asked, hands still guiding her hips, mouth at her throat. "Before I stopped you."

"Everything."

"What were you gonna do, once you got me out?"

Laurel swallowed. "Suck your cock."

A curt moan answered her and his hands gripped tighter, nearly too much. A breath before she could ask him to be gentler, he let her go. "On your knees."

I know that voice. She made her way to the cold floor once more. That voice belonged to a man she'd met last summer, a stranger named Flynn who'd invited her to this very apartment and showed her all the frightening things he liked in bed. A man who'd professed not to spoon and not to call women after he'd messed around with them. In time he'd proven himself a liar on both counts, but the man with her tonight... This could've been their first time together, for how familiar he felt just now.

He sat on the couch. Laurel knew better than to stroke his thighs or go for his fly as she had earlier—not without say-so. This Flynn was in charge, and she'd do only what he asked. What he commanded.

"Show me what you were gonna do, girl."

She dipped her chin in a tiny nod. She reached for his belt, unthreading it slowly, her body buzzing, hands nearly shaking. She felt as nervous as she had their first night alone together, but just as excited. Wet, too. Ready for whatever he demanded of her.

She spread the thick leather of his belt and opened the button of his fly, then the zipper. Merino wool teased her knuckles, the sweater she'd chosen for a man she'd known so well, worn now by this thrilling and unnerving stranger. It was so soft, the body beneath it merciless and hard. She let the feelings move through her like a song hummed out of tune. Any fear she felt was welcome, a dark new shadow in a forest she tread in fearlessly.

"Take me out. Get me hard."

She knew those words as a penitent woman might know a Bible verse. She tugged his jeans low and he shifted, pushing them to his hips. The second half of his order proved moot; his erection looked obscene even through black cotton, and again Laurel felt that prickle in her mouth, thirst spiking. She stroked him with the heel of her hand, but he wanted more. He pushed his waistband down, exposing every ready inch. The breath left her in a huff.

"That what you wanted to see?"

She nodded, meeting his eyes. "Yes."

"Stroke it."

She wrapped her hand around that fevered flesh. His pulse throbbed in her grip, impatient. Insistent. She kept it slow, kept it tight, measuring him with her fist. His scent was so strong now. She'd find his excitement gleaming at his slit before long, evidence of his need so like the wetness already slicking her lips.

"You like that?"

"Yes."

"Tell me."

"I love your cock." *I love you, exactly like this.* It was like loving a stranger—impulsive and thrilling.

"Show me how much you love it."

She gripped his root and lowered her mouth. He tasted as he smelled, potent and personal. She swallowed him halfway—as much as she could without gagging. Then again, again, stroking the underside with her tongue, letting his head nearly slip from her lips only to claim him again, a little deeper, a little deeper still.

"More."

I know what you want. What every man wanted, it often felt, but only this one had ever managed to make sexy, as far as Laurel was concerned. Words from three seasons back echoed in her ears—spoken to another woman but meant for her. Of that she had no doubt.

Good girl. I wanna see you choke on that cock.

She gave what he asked. Slid her lips past the point of comfort and his crown bumped her palate, triggering that first reflexive gag. She felt the spasm but not the sting in her sinuses, not the roiling in her stomach. She knew this act too well.

A cool, heavy hand came to rest on the nape of her neck, sending a shiver trickling down her back. She took him deep again, reveling in the way her muscles clenched, unafraid. While the sensation wasn't strictly pleasant, the result was reward enough to go there, tenfold. She might tense with every fresh violation, but it was nothing compared to how her reaction affected him.

Like an electrical pulse, his entire body jerked each time she gagged. Sometimes a "yeah" or a "fuck" rewarded her, sometimes a half-swallowed moan. Her mouth was awash with spit, a reflex she'd once found embarrassing, but now welcomed part and parcel with the rest of this act. It bathed his flesh and eased the motions, slipped from her lips in warm ribbons. It made her feel sloppy but that only sharpened the taboo. The biology of his desire was ugly, and these were the things that turned him on like nothing else. She welcomed the wet heat as it slid along her jugular, welcomed his deepening moans as his hips began to work.

The hand on her neck moved to her hair, fisting her ponytail. "Take that cock. Nice and deep. Show me how bad you fucking want it."

Held this way, her chance to own some part of this act was gone. Her only options now were to submit or to flee, and that choice needed no deliberation.

In time she felt her face flushing, her nose growing runny. Just as she was beginning to hope he'd finish soon, he eased her off him by her hair. She sat back on her knees, resisting an urge to sniff, or to flex her aching jaw. She kept her eyes on his chest, watching its quick rise and fall and awaiting whatever came next.

"On my bed," he ordered, face and voice both cold as January.

She got to her feet, legs tingly. She could feel his eyes on her every step of the way, found them studying her hips or thighs when she turned and sat. His cock was hidden by his shorts once more. He fisted his jeans and belt and approached, stopping before her, seeming mountainous. He peeled away his sweater and undershirt in one pull, then slid his belt free with a slow, smooth motion. It looked like a bullwhip in his fist. He tossed it behind her on the bed. She'd expected him to keep his jeans on, but he pushed them down along with his shorts, stepping free of the pile and stripping his socks. Usually when he was playing the cold and controlling stranger, he kept his pants on. It seemed that power play wasn't needed tonight, and it made her wonder exactly who this was.

Whoever he might be, he looked powerful and impenetrable even without of stitch of clothing hiding that pale skin. Whatever he might

CARA McKENNA

want, it was as dark as his shaded eyes or the hair framing his ready cock, or the stitches marring his brow.

"Take your top off."

She undid each button on her blouse, revealing a plum-colored bra patterned in white vines. Her panties matched. She'd dressed as she'd felt only hours ago—womanly, sexy, confident. She couldn't say what she felt now or what underwear would best embody it, only that this wasn't quite right.

"Your bra," he said.

Reaching back, she freed the hooks. She let the straps fall from her arms just as he reached down to grab one of her legs. He lifted it, unzipping her boot, sliding it off. It hit the floor with a thump, a little jangle of its decorative buckle. Next came her sock. Again, on the other side. If it excited him, that face didn't give away a thing.

She expected her skirt to come next, but he said, "Hands and knees."

She obeyed, moving to the middle of the mattress on all fours. The belt was there, close enough to touch if she splayed her fingers, and she doubted its presence was accidental.

His weight shifted the mattress beneath her, an ages-old trigger that had anticipation winding tight inside her. Heavy hands sought her thighs then rose, pushing her skirt up, kneading her ass, her hips, roaming along her sides and ribs and finally cupping her breasts. He taunted with grazing caresses of his calloused, workingman's palms, then mean tweaks of her nipples. She gasped from the pleasure and pain equally, that balance he could navigate like a tightrope walker.

Her skirt had fallen back into place and he shoved it roughly up to her waist. His thumbs slid under the hems of her underwear, bunching the fabric into a strip between her cheeks. She waited for it—the first spank. Instead she got his short nails dragging over her skin, then the teasing, pleasurably demeaning sensation of her panties being pushed up farther, wedged tight in her cleft, damp cotton cleaving her labia.

"You look good, girl."

She swallowed.

"You wet for me?"

"Yes."

"Gimme the belt."

She passed it back, nerves flashing cold, then hot.

"All the way down."

A familiar order. She lowered, laying her shoulders and one side of her face on the sheet. The rumpled cotton smelled of Flynn, of both of them, and she extended her arms back along her sides. A muscle in her neck whined as he brought her wrists together at the small of her back and wrapped them in the leather. It had always been an awkward position for her, but she settled into the discomfort as she'd learned to. There was a tug as he secured the buckle, then he let her hands go.

He pulled her underwear down some but didn't take them off. Instead he yanked the crotch to one side, and there it was—the smooth, blunt head of his cock, seeking entrance. She was mindful to take a deep breath and release it slowly, to will her body to relax. She'd been crampy on and off since she'd had the IUD put in, and she didn't relish that pain on top of the contortion.

"Yeah," he muttered, pushing inside. "So fucking wet." He wasn't patient, but as he sank in fully on the third thrust, her body settled without a twinge. He felt obscene, the thick intrusion of his cock underscoring the scent of the sheets, the sounds of his deepening grunts, the true bondage of her wrists and the added constriction of her twisted panties.

Laurel had a private name for this sensation—*trussed*. It unleashed a flurry of emotions when they took things here, the experience at once humiliating and exhilarating. The sort of thing she might glimpse in pornography and find both demeaning and titillating, but on balance feel too squicked by to keep watching. The sort of thing she'd always held against a lover, should she discover it was his taste. Until Flynn.

He was so up front, so guileless, his desires didn't threaten her. She followed him places she never would have imagined she might, never bumping up against a kink that didn't repay her discomfort at least twofold in pleasure or gratification.

At least not until tonight. As the thrill of the initial penetration faded, her excitement ebbed, outshone by a growing strain in her shoulder, a nagging itch where the wool of her skirt's waist rubbed her skin. A nagging *worry* in her head, one she'd never encountered in this bed before.

Even deep inside her body, he felt so far away. It made her ache to free her wrists and turn over, to wrap her arms around him, hold him tight. But that was merely what *she* wanted. What he needed tonight looked far different, but she'd give him that all the same. She'd endure it, and come out sore and probably uncertain, but not hurt. Not where it counted. Under all the worry, she felt strong. Strong enough to be whatever release he needed. Strong enough to trust this was still the same man she loved, even as he felt undeniably like a stranger.

She was sweating now, the wool chafing, the elastic of her panties pulled taut against the seam of one thigh and promising a mark. She shoved those details aside and instead pictured his face, cheeks stained dark with effort, eyes at once wild and stony, lips parted and flushed. The image struck that flint deep inside her belly, the first spark that told her an orgasm was possible. It'd take more though, and it felt foolish to hope that her pleasure was on his mind, tonight.

"You feel good," he told her again, his voice like water to a woman lost in a desert. She drank the words down, dying for more.

"I want to plea—ease you," she said, jolted by his hammering hips.

"You do nothing tonight but get fucked." His reply was coarse but quenching all the same.

"Yes, Sir." She hadn't called him that in ages. The formality of it had always seemed corny to Laurel, but it felt right tonight, somehow. She'd read a book about D/s sex after they'd become a couple. Was this subspace? Wait, no—she was thinking far too much for that. She was thinking far too much, period. She needed more. She needed pleasure to let her endure the discomfort. And there was no choice but to spell it out for him.

"I want to come for you."

His hips kept pumping but his sounds changed, grunts muted to huffs of air. "That so?"

"Yes, please. On your cock, just like this."

"Beg me again. Beg me again, and maybe I'll give you exactly what you need."

"Please, Sir. Touch me, please. I want it so bad it hurts." She wanted it so badly, just to balance out the hurt.

"You want my touch," he echoed, his tone maybe mocking, maybe just cocky. One hand moved from her hip to her crack, thumb drawing a shocking line down and over her hole.

Her breath was gone, body tossed between misgiving and excitement, as it always was when he took liberties back there. He reached around to wet his thumb where his driving cock met her slick lips. He swept his fingertips over her clit for a single second's torturous tease before returning to her ass.

She gave herself over to this moment, still intimidating after all this time with Flynn, but familiar. The faint sting of the intrusion, the warped pleasure of the transgression. It wasn't the touch she craved, but there was no denying it solidified the need pulsing in her belly.

"That what you wanted?" he demanded.

"I'll take whatever you give me."

His thumb twisted, retreated, delved deep again, feeling better by the second. "Good answer. But don't lie to me, sweetheart."

"I wouldn't."

"Tell me what you want." Such words could have felt reassuring, except he sounded cold, so cold.

"My clit," she mumbled.

"Tell me."

"My clit. Please. Please."

He shifted, knocking her knees wider with his own for balance, then inching the hand still holding her hip forward, seeking her cunt.

She cried out the moment he glanced that blazing, aching spot. There was a spit-damp patch of sheet spreading under her cheek. Her neck was wrenched and her hands were numb, screaming for blood, but all at once she felt none of it. The universe shrank to the point where his fingertips met her clit, blinding bright, nearly too much to bear.

She moaned like a crazy woman when he stroked her there, suddenly breathing so fast she could be hyperventilating. "God. Please."

"Say my name."

"Flynn. Fuck, *please*, Flynn."

He gave her exactly what she needed—tight, rough circles falling into sync with his punishing cock, his plundering thumb.

She was long gone, half-aware of the mantra of her voice, a pitiful chant of "Please, please, please." Mere seconds and she was moaning, trembling, begging with every cell in her body.

"Good girl. Come on that cock."

It was that familiar praise that did her in, plummeting her headlong into oblivion.

Through the quaking of her release she felt him succumb to his own. His cock drove as deep as it went, fingers digging into her hips and promising bruises. Any pain she endured was worth the price to feel the familiar rhythm of his hips as he emptied inside her, to hear the pained groans as pleasure turned him helpless.

Their bodies fell still, rocked in tiny frissons by their pumping hearts and gulping lungs. When he pulled out, Laurel felt the dirty-sweet heat of their mingled sex wetting her savaged panties.

He stretched out on his back, eyes shut, one arm cocked above his head. Laurel got up to use the bathroom and abandon the last of her clothes. When she joined him on the bed, she was spent enough to not overthink things and to take what she wanted—contact. Skin to skin, so quiet after the force of the storm.

She laid her arm across his chest, feeling his heart beating under her palm, under his warm, slick skin. So close, and yet he still felt miles away.

"I miss you," she whispered.

"What's that mean?"

"You feel so far away… I understand why. I'm not asking you to be any different. But I miss you all the same."

"I need time."

"You can have all you want. Do you need space?"

"I dunno yet."

"You can have that too. Just say."

"I don't know what I need. I'm not used to being this fucking…" He struggled for the right word.

"Vulnerable?" Laurel hazarded, just as he settled on, "Torn up."

She held him tighter.

"I'm gonna tell you something right now," he said, "and I want you to remember it every time I'm angry with you, for as long as we're together."

"All right."

"I wouldn't be this ripped up if I didn't love you. I don't waste my time feeling pissed or hurt or let down unless the person who managed to make me feel it actually matters to me."

"Okay." She wished it were more of a consolation.

"I'm not looking to change anything we've got. I just need to figure out what the fuck's up with me. Or to sit and stew in it for however long it takes me to get over it."

She nodded.

"You're stuck with me," he said, "same as always. Even if I decide I need some space. You prepared to believe that?"

Again she nodded, hoping it was true. No matter what he told her, if they took some time apart she'd never quit worrying if he might decide to end things. Not for a minute. She trusted him with her life, but this felt like another matter entirely.

Still, she'd suck it up and play it cool, if that was what he needed.

Even if inside she'd be dying anew every hour of the day.

CHAPTER ELEVEN

FLYNN LAY AWAKE FOR AGES after Laurel dropped off, mind buzzing despite the release, flitting from resentment to guilt and back, endlessly, the latter steadily eclipsing the former.

He wasn't proud of what had happened tonight.

Though he didn't doubt Laurel had been up for it, even enjoyed it... He shouldn't have gone there. His kink was barbaric, the sex he liked best cruel and crass, but he'd never done that before—let his true emotions feed his fantasies. It felt unmistakably disturbing in the wake of the orgasm. Shame settled around him like a bad odor, one he'd not caught a whiff of in ages.

It was tempting to blame the alcohol, but too easy. Too cowardly. It was all on him. No matter how badly he'd needed the relief of sex, he shouldn't have taken things there, not while he'd been upset with her. It didn't matter that she'd welcomed it, or that she'd not used their safe word, or that she'd come. What mattered was how different it had felt, and if he'd picked up on that, there was no doubt she had as well. Normally when they got rough he wouldn't hesitate to slap her ass or her thighs, call her a bitch or a cunt or any other mean thing, but something had held him back. He'd known it would've been wrong, feeling the way he had. That should've been warning enough. Even with consent, even with a history as intimate as theirs, there were limits within the limits. He'd stopped short of the harshest ones, but it didn't make him feel any more justified now that his sweat and come had cooled.

He'd brought actual anger into bed with them. He *felt* actual anger toward her still, and laying here stewing in it with her body so close felt as toxic as the guilt.

He slipped from the covers and found his jeans and sweater in the dark, got his boots laced in the strips of light slipping in between the window blinds. He scrawled a note by the glow of the microwave clock. *On the roof. Need to think.* He set it atop his pillow, hoping she wouldn't find occasion to read it, or to discover he'd left her.

He locked up and headed for the stairwell, hiked all the way up until the steps went from carpeted concrete to clanging metal, ending at the heavy door that led out onto the roof. It was never locked, though tonight it was ajar to boot. He pushed it out, welcomed a cool breeze on his face.

It smelled like spring. Like spring and…menthols. He glanced upwind, to the frayed folding lawn chair propped at the building's far corner. A tumble of wavy auburn hair moved with the wind, seeming to snatch at the blue smoke drifting in Flynn's direction. He crossed the roof.

"Heather."

She whipped around, peering at him over the back of the chair. "Mike, Jesus. You fuckin' scared me. What're you doin' up here so late?"

He sat on the ledge opposite her, planting his elbows on his knees. "Could ask you the same thing."

"New Year's resolution—no more smoking indoors. I figure I'll smoke less if I have to come all the way up here." She had a glass of wine in one hand, ashed her butt with the other. "Plus the landlord's been on my ass."

"You know it's March, right?"

"It was too cold to start in January."

He rolled his eyes but couldn't hold back a smile. "Good for you."

"Now you. What're you up here for?"

"I dunno. Just needed some space."

"Laurel sleeping over?"

He nodded.

"Get your ass off that ledge. Makes me fucking itchy."

He moved to sit on the roof itself, back against the short wall.

Heather took a drag, eyes narrowed at him. "You two all right?"

"Yeah. I think so."

"You think?"

"She's fine. She's just about over it. You know, the pregnancy and all that."

"The miscarriage."

He winced. "Yeah. That."

"And what about you?"

Flynn shrugged. "I'm glad she's feeling better."

"You're such a lousy fuckin' liar."

"It's true." He was glad Laurel felt better. He just still felt like shit himself, was all.

She sipped her wine. "For real—why're you up here, Mike?"

"I dunno. Couldn't sleep."

"Is one of you pissed at the other?"

He shrugged again, as good as nodding to someone who knew him as well as his sister did.

"Who?"

"Me. At her. Not pissed, though. Just… Fuck if I know. Annoyed, maybe."

"About what?"

"Just… I dunno. That she's over it, and it feels like I'm stuck back where we were two weeks ago. And annoyed because she still has no goddamn idea what she would've done about it, if the pregnancy hadn't ended."

"Why's that annoying?"

"Because how the fuck do you *not know?* How do you lose a baby that way and not realize afterward what you felt about it?"

"Because miscarriage is fuckin' confusing as shit," Heather said, and took another long pull off her cigarette. "Take it from me. I had three—two babies I wasn't ready for and another I really goddamn wanted. You feel everything, no matter what you think you should be feeling. You feel guilty and sad and responsible, every fuckin' thing."

"Laurel said she felt relieved."

"Of course she did. It made the decision for her. I don't blame her—it's bound to be a shitty-ass choice to make. So what did you feel?"

"Sad."

"And relieved?"

"No, not really. Just sad. And a little angry."

"At Laurel?"

"No, of course not." And was he actually angry at her now? Not really. What he felt was *betrayed,* only it wasn't. He felt left behind. He still felt lost, and she was busy finding normal again. Better than normal, even.

"So what're you really angry at, then?" Heather demanded.

He huffed a big, noisy breath, annoyed all over again at this interrogation. "Like I even know… Just mad she had to go through that. Mad that she got her decision taken away from her."

"Mad she didn't get to decide."

"That's what I said."

"Mad that fate made the call, and she was helpless to do anything about it."

"Sure."

Heather smiled in the dimness and a car honked down in the street. "*You* feel helpless."

"Maybe," he allowed, rankled.

"Of course you do. And of course that fuckin' hurts. Every other thing in your life, you get some say in it. Even in the pregnancy— Laurel would've let you speak your piece if you'd been willing to. But then losing it? *That*, you had zero control of."

He made a face, thinking she was on to something but not happy to admit it.

"You couldn't *protect it*," Heather said, marking the thought with a stabbing motion of her glowing butt in his direction, squinting with triumph or maybe just from the smoke. "That's your currency in this life, Mike. You're the strong one. The one who takes no shit, and takes care of the people you love. That tiny little speck in her belly— you couldn't protect that."

"I don't even know if I wanted her to keep it, necessarily." That was true, despite what he'd told Laurel in the heat of the moment.

"No, but that doesn't matter, see? Even if Laurel had decided to get an abortion, that was still in your control, because you gave her your blessing, whatever she decided, right?"

"Yeah. I suppose."

"But neither of you got to decide. It just went *poof*. And that stole away your power."

He nodded, grudgingly accepting that Heather might have him pegged. He didn't like thinking that anybody had a better handle on his shit than he did, but her words had loosened something that'd been knotted up inside him.

It wasn't the baby he was mourning, was it? Heather was right. It was the control he felt robbed of.

So what did you do? Fucked your girlfriend like a stranger you couldn't give two shits about. That wasn't his way, not even with an actual one-night stand. Flynn might be a sick fucker, but he was a gentleman, in his way.

Not tonight, I wasn't. Tonight he'd been the sort of man he'd be more than happy to punch in the mouth.

He leaned forward, gesturing for Heather's cigarette. "Gimme a taste of that."

"No fuckin' chance." She sucked the final gasp of life out of the butt and crushed its corpse under her sneaker, tar paper grinding. She drained her glass and stood, stretching. "The thing is, Mike, all this shit you're going through? That's how kids work. From the second they're conceived, you're pretty much fucked."

He laughed, just a little hum of a thing, but it felt good. Another couple tangles came loose in his chest.

"All bets are off with kids," Heather said, "whether they're Kim's age or they're a little blob of cells. Hell, you're basically my kid and you're fuckin' thirty-three and I still can't sleep on weekend nights, knowin' you're playing chicken with brain damage in that goddamned basement—"

"I got it."

"Anyhow, the little cell-blob decided for you. You want kids someday, get used to havin' fuck-all control. Second you start carin' about somebody on that level is the second you hand all your ammo over to them, throw out your arms, invite 'em to take aim straight at your heart."

She offered a hand to help Flynn up but he shook his head. "Gonna stay up here a little while longer."

"Suit yourself. She know where you are?"

"I left a note."

"She know you're pissed?"

"Yeah. Probably." Flynn was unpracticed at hiding his feelings; he said what he thought, never censored himself. That little speech he'd made after the sex couldn't have been all that reassuring.

"She finds that note, she's gonna start worrying," his sister said. "Maybe start wonderin' what she did wrong, as us fool-ass women are programmed to do. Don't make her worry a minute longer than she has to."

He nodded.

She tousled his hair in that way he hated, that way he'd miss like oxygen if she was somehow gone tomorrow. "Night, kid."

"Night."

He watched her go. He ought to move to the chair, but the roof felt right under his ass, cold and hard and awkward. All the things he'd been to Laurel, tonight.

She's gonna start worrying. Yeah, probably. Being a dick on occasion was one thing, but tonight had been something else entirely. It'd be selfish to stay up here, wallowing, knowing if she woke he'd only wind up hurting her more.

He got to his feet, feeling old and achy, feeling every hit he'd ever taken and every hour he'd ever labored in his muscles and bones and heart, and deserving every pang. He crossed the roof, scanning the city, feeling as determined as he did lost as he hauled the door open and stepped inside.

Two flights down, he unlocked the apartment as quietly as he could, toed off his boots and shed his jacket and sweater and jeans. As his eyes adjusted, he looked to the bed. The note sat where he'd left it atop his pillow. Laurel had moved though, turned over, her pale arm slung across the dark bedspread. He should have been here, should have felt the sweet weight of that arm as it sought him in the dark.

Too fucking bad. He couldn't fix that lost chance, not any more than he could've fixed things when she'd lost the pregnancy. If control really was what he valued, it was the present he ought to be focused on.

He crept around the bed, grabbed the note and crumpled it into a ball, small and hard as a marble, and tossed it in the trash under the sink. He used the bathroom and washed his hands, ran a wet washcloth over his face. The fan sounded so loud, his thoughts so quiet at long last.

The sheets were warm as he slid beneath the covers on Laurel's side of the bed.

"Hey," he whispered, seeking her body, his chest meeting her back.

"Mm." A pause. "You're freezing."

"I needed the can." Not a lie, thankfully.

"You smell like cigarettes."

He didn't reply, grateful she was half asleep.

"Want me to budge over?"

Though he was wedged on a narrow sliver of mattress, he said, "No. Stay right here." He wrapped his arm tight around her, warmed through when her hand covered his at her heart.

She said nothing for a long time, but he could tell from the subtle tension in her body, she wasn't asleep. Finally she whispered, "You back?"

She didn't mean back in the apartment. He knew precisely what she meant.

"Yeah, I'm back."

"Good."

"Sorry I left."

"Don't be sorry. Just don't go away again."

"I won't," he promised. "Now get some sleep, honey."

CHAPTER TWELVE

WITH THE HELP OF HIS SISTER'S SMOKE-SCENTED WISDOM, Flynn slowly came to accept that maybe it wasn't so sad and pointless, the way things had happened with the baby. Like maybe surrender was just the price you paid when pregnancy and kids entered the picture. He was pretty useless at surrendering, but the thought was comforting in its way. It became his first step toward moving on.

He and Laurel saw each other less than usual the next couple weeks, but not infrequently. If he woke up angry at the world on a given morning, he let her know he needed space that night. He'd finish work and toil in the gym for twice as long as usual, pound his angst into the bags or sweat it onto the bench, mop it away with a towel. He tried not to take it to bed with him. Mostly succeeded.

It was a warm Monday afternoon at the start of April when he noticed the biggest change—he'd gone an entire workday without thinking about any of it. A long, laborious slog of a day spent tacking drywall in Fort Point, an industrial vent droning nearby and making conversation with his coworkers impossible, infinite opportunities to ruminate and dwell…and yet he hadn't. He'd thought about a thousand other things—baseball, a beef with his boss, the taxes he couldn't put off much longer—but not the lost pregnancy.

He called Laurel on his way to the gym to ask if she wanted to hang out that night, but it went to voicemail after a single ring. "Hey, it's me. Calling to see if you wanna stay over tonight. Lemme know." He pocketed his phone and cut down the alley beside the bar, exchanged a curt nod of greeting with a fellow boxer as he emerged from the side door. Flynn caught it just as it was about to swing shut and headed down the steps.

He felt the buzz of his phone as he was shedding his jacket and checked the screen. Laurel. "Hey, hang on a sec." The reception downstairs sucked.

"Sure," came her crackly reply.

He headed for the stairwell, trotting back up and out into the alley. "Okay, I'm good. Had to get out of the dungeon. You get my message?"

"I did. Sorry I missed you—I was on the subway." Her voice was hitching slightly.

"You walkin' someplace?"

"Yeah. Anyway, I'd love to hang out."

"I could pick you up about seven," he said, eyeing the sky. He was in a tee and the hairs on his arms were prickling in the cold. It felt like rain, but he didn't care. His own forecast was fair, at long last. "I was thinkin' maybe we could swing by the grocery store on the way back, grab a rotisserie chicken or something."

"Yum. I could make mashed potatoes."

"It's a plan."

A pause. "You sound different," Laurel said slyly. "You have a good day?"

"Nothin' special. Just feeling more like normal, I guess."

"Glad to hear it. And you look nice in that shirt."

He frowned, lost.

A laugh came through the line. "Look up, Flynn."

He did, spotting a redhead in jeans and an olive jacket heading his way, a familiar purple umbrella under one arm. He smiled and switched off his phone. "On the subway, huh? What the fuck're you doin' here?"

She slid her own phone into her purse as she reached him and leaned up for a kiss. "Coming to see you."

"You're lucky I'm so predictable." The first raindrop fell, hitting him on his bare biceps. "Should I grab my shit? You got other plans for me?"

"I do, but they won't take long. You can still torture yourself as scheduled."

"You got my curiosity piqued, honey. What's up?"

"Firstly, I have news." And good news, to judge by the smile she was failing to hold in.

She'd had a second interview at that biotech place a good week and a half ago. After all that silence, she'd begun insisting they must not want her, but he'd kept shushing her, reminding her it took a while to check references. And that they'd be retarded not to hire her.

"That company call you back, finally?" he asked.

"They did indeed."

"And?"

She didn't say anything, just smiled a mile wide and nodded so hard her hair bounced.

"Laurel, that is fucking fantastic." He hauled her against him, jabbed in the ribs by her umbrella but not caring. He rocked her back and forth, probably squeezed the life half out of her, but he couldn't let go. He just wanted to smell her hair and memorize the smothered laughter warming the base of his throat. Fuck, she'd waited a long time for this.

He let her go, grinning as he took her in, almost like it was the first time. "Holy shit. You really did it, huh?"

"I guess I did."

"When do you start?"

"A couple weeks." She was glowing, practically hovering off the asphalt. He didn't think he'd ever seen this version of Laurel. He wondered what he could do to make her acquaintance more often.

"I'll go in and fill out some paperwork before then, but my official first day is April seventeenth."

"Jesus, fuck the chicken—lemme take you someplace nice, tonight."

"No, no. I want exactly what you said. It's so dreary out, let's hunker down inside."

"Your call. But you're getting a party, whether you like it or not. Second I tell Heather the news is the second she'll start callin' to ask what your favorite dessert is."

"I'll look forward to that." Laurel changed then, her smile suddenly more shy than exuberant. Little droplets of rain were gathering in her hair, shiny like dew. Flynn could feel them dampening his tee and spiking his eyelashes. He reached for her umbrella, ripping the Velcro strap free and popping it open to hand over.

"Thanks." Definitely shy. No mistaking it.

"You got somethin' else to say?" he asked.

She pursed her lips, took a breath in, a breath out. She set the umbrella down. It lolled in the breeze, collecting the mounting rain. He was about to stoop and grab it when she blurted, "I do. I have something else to say."

"All right. Better make it snappy if that purse is real leather."

"I have something to ask you," she clarified, looking not at his face, but at some nowhere spot on his chest.

"Shoot."

She dropped down, kneeling.

Flynn's head gave a shake, a little spasm of surprise. It wasn't the first time she'd dropped to her knees before him, but for one thing they weren't in his apartment, and for another she was on one knee, not two. His eyes grew wide. "Whoa."

Laurel cleared her throat officiously. "I kneel before you as a woman with her shit finally together," she said, her hair wet now, gathering in long, slick waves, sticking to her cheeks. She tucked them behind her ears and met his stare. "I know you would've taken me as a woman with her shit still falling apart, but that's not how I wanted to do this. And you don't always get your way."

"Honey," was all he could think to say.

She reached into her jacket pocket, then there in her open palm sat a ring.

"Michael Flynn," she began, voice breaking. She composed herself, blowing out a breath. "Will you marry me in approximately two years?"

A noiseless laugh jerked his shoulders and a smile spread across his lips. "You know I will. You sure you'll be ready by then?"

"Well, I'm not done. Michael *Paul* Flynn, will you make me the happiest woman in Boston and drive my U-Haul when I move out of my apartment and into yours when my lease is up at the end of May?"

He laughed for real at that, feeling high and confused, but also pretty fucking delighted. Rain was soaking his shirt, trickling down the hollow of his back, but it was hard to believe; it felt so exactly like a sunny summer's day.

"Yes, I will. Now stand the fuck up."

She did, holding out the ring. It was a thick silver band, brushed, not shiny.

"How'd you know my size?"

"I didn't. The guy at the store said I can exchange it if it doesn't fit. Try it on."

He slipped it on his left ring finger but it got stuck at the second knuckle. He modeled it anyhow, angling his hand this way and that, making her giggle.

"Guess they didn't take me seriously enough when I said you have huge hands." She tugged it free and slipped it back into her pocket.

"How'd you know I wouldn't prefer gold?" he teased.

"Titanium seemed the butchest choice."

"When you put it like that."

"Seriously, would you like something different?"

He reached out and cupped her cold, wet jaw, kissed her mouth as the rain ran down their faces. "No," he said as he let her go. "I want whatever you pick out for me. You really wanna move in with me?"

She nodded. "Only time will tell if it feels like enough space once we're in each other's faces twenty-four-seven—"

"Faces and pants."

"—but if we can swing it, it'd save a lot on rent. I mean, it'd be nice to own a place before…you know. Before a baby came along. Someday."

"Sure." He stooped for her umbrella, shaking the water out of it and holding it over their heads.

"Plus I want to make sure you have a chance to see what it's like to be with me, full time. Because of my depression, I mean."

"Oh?"

"Don't get me wrong," she said, "you've been awesome for as long as we've been together. But it's exhausting living with someone when they're going through mental-health crap. Trust me, my mom taught me well."

He nodded, thinking of the years Heather had spent suffering through Robbie's shit after he'd come home from Iraq. PTSD made Laurel's struggles look like a rained-out ballgame.

"The meds are helping," she added. "Plus I won't have the job guilt nagging at me for a change. Maybe I'm worrying too much. Maybe the future's all glitter and butterflies."

"A future you'll be sharing with me," he said, cocky.

"That's the plan, it would seem."

"So, does anything else need to change, if you're gonna be my old lady, officially?"

She frowned. "Like what?"

He nodded toward the bar's side door. "You need to lay down the law about me getting punched in the head every week, maybe?"

"What, make you quit fighting? Jesus, that'd be mean. No."

"No?" He'd been expecting such an ultimatum, if not happy about it.

"One depressed person in a couple is plenty. You do what keeps you sane." She studied his arm, the one holding the umbrella. "And insanely fit."

"Good to hear."

"Were you worried I'd tell you to quit?"

"Not worried, exactly. But Heather's always told me I better knock that shit off if I expect any rational woman to commit to my ass."

"I don't know what that says about me, but I don't think I could ever ask you to stop fighting. Not unless you were getting concussed. I do like your brain the way it is."

"You sure? 'Cause it's got some terrible ideas about what I'm gonna do to you, later."

"I love it all the more, then." She paused, distracted by the motion-sensor light that had blinked on above them—the weather had brought dusk early this evening. "Well, I've said everything I came here to. Why don't you finish up downstairs, and I'll get on top of dinner, and I'll see you whenever you get home?"

That sounded so bizarre—doing something as mundane as his daily workout with all this news to process. "Not a bad idea. I'll probably need an hour alone for it to sink in that I'm fucking engaged."

She laughed. "You and me both. Okay, better say bye before we drown out here. See you in a bit. Hopefully my future apartment will smell like something delicious by the time you get home."

He gave her a kiss, both their sets of lips chilly, his hand feeling stiff and clumsy as he passed her umbrella back. "I love you so fucking much," he murmured, letting her hear how fiercely he meant it, letting her see it in his face. "I hope you know that."

She nodded. "I do."

"I'll show you exactly how much when I get home."

Pink warmed her pale cheeks and she smiled. "I'll look forward to that."

He let the rain pelt him as he watched her walk away, down the alley and around the corner. When she was out of sight he punched in the code for the door and headed downstairs. He stripped off his shirt and wrung it out, laid it over a radiator to dry. As he began his warm up, jogging in place, he tried that word on for size again in his head. *Engaged.* When he got home tonight he'd open up his lockbox and slip that ring on her finger, finally. And soon enough the cat would be out of the bag.

How did you propose? Heather would want to know.

In the middle of the miscarriage. She said no.

Well, how did she *propose, then?*

In the rain, in an alley next to a dive bar. I said yes.

He smiled to himself, thinking that was just about perfect, somehow.

* * *

Laurel turned at the sound of the deadbolt, a smile cracking her face wide open, too broad and goofy to possibly hide.

"Hello," she called. She was busy at the counter, wearing pajama pants while her jeans tumbled dry five flights below in one of the building's coin-op machines.

Flynn stepped inside, looking soaked to the bone. "Smells amazing."

"I stole your idea—we're having rotisserie chicken. And risotto and veggies. You look like you swam here."

"Feels like I did." He unlaced his boots, rain dripping from his hood when he leaned over. "But you won't catch me complaining—if it ain't snow, it's fine by me." He stripped to his shorts right there, leaving his clothes in a pile—or perhaps a puddle—by the door. And giving any neighbors across the street a free thrill, as the blinds were up.

He stopped by the counter on his way to the bathroom, kissing Laurel's cheek with icy lips and eyeing the cutting board.

"Carrots."

"And broccoli and zucchini." She ran her palm over his wet hair and his cheek. "Good God, you're freezing. Get in the shower."

"You want your ring?"

"I can wait." She wondered if he could guess that she'd spent a good ten minutes poking fruitlessly around in his drawers and filing cabinet, trying to find it. "Go get warmed up."

"You make a bossy fiancée."

She started. "Oh my God, I hadn't even thought of that. *Fiancée*."

"How about that? Earned yourself two fancy-ass new titles in one day."

"I guess so."

He headed for the bathroom and Laurel's shit-eating grin bloomed anew. He'd find more than the relief of a steaming shower in there—she'd slung the old red towel over the rod. The note on the mirror read, simply, *Whatever you want.*

She'd better hold off on starting the risotto. It'd only wind up a gluey mess if Flynn decided to take her up on that invitation the second he stepped out of the bathroom. She finished chopping the veggies, lowered the blinds and got comfy on the bed, studying the apartment. She bet she could convince the landlord to let her paint the walls. Heather's place was painted. It might take the edge off the starkness of the space—

The bathroom door swung in and the fan and light flipped off. "Whatever I want?" Flynn asked as he appeared. The red towel was knotted around his waist.

She nodded. "Whatever you want."

He walked to the closet. "What I want," he said, opening the door and reaching up to the top shelf, "is for you to wear something very special, tonight."

Her eyebrows rose. Flynn wasn't the lingerie type. Then the surprise changed to confusion when he turned, holding a gray box as big as a milk crate—a safe.

"What— Oh." The ring, duh. "I'll have you know I looked all over for that, while you were out."

He set the box on the bed and crossed the room to unhook his keys from his abandoned pants. "That rock's worth more than everything else in this apartment put together," he said, opening the safe. "This shoulda been the first place you looked."

And there it was—from the big gray box came the tiny, gleaming wooden one. He sat at her side and popped it open. Just one glance at the diamond and her breath was gone, sucked clean out of her lungs.

"Wow."

"You finally gonna put it on?"

She nodded, mesmerized.

He slid it free and held it out. Laurel accepted it with a surprisingly calm hand, studying it by the light of the reading lamp. "I have a job and a diamond ring," she whispered.

"That you do. Put it on."

"Aren't you supposed to do it?"

"Am I?"

She shrugged. "That's what they do in movies." She was stalling, feeling tears brewing, emotion rising like a tide.

"As you wish." He took it and Laurel offered her ring finger, unable to hold back a sloppy, quavering smile as he slid it on. It couldn't have been a better fit.

Laurel had never been the type to lie around daydreaming about proposals or rings or weddings or babies, but it was undeniably powerful, this moment. Like stumbling across a threshold into a new stage of womanhood.

"Nice work, Anne," Flynn said.

"Ha, indeed. I'll have to take her out for a seriously overpriced dinner when my first engineering paycheck clears." She angled her hand this way and that, watched the light dancing in the stone. "Jesus, it's so beautiful."

"Glad you like it."

She paused her ogling long enough to pull him in for a kiss. Then another, another, probably a dozen before she finally let him go. "Wow. Thank you."

"Thanks for proposing. Saved me a lot of anxiety."

"I was a little worried you'd be all old school about it. About the dude doing the asking, I mean."

He shook his head. "Long as I still wear the pants in bed, I'm easy."

She laughed, then looked to his bare torso. "You're currently wearing nothing but a highly contentious towel. What comes first—dinner or depravity?"

"Seems pointless to get dressed, only to get naked again in a half hour."

"Very well. What're you in the mood for?"

"You'll find out as soon as you get your clothes off."

She stood, smirking, and made a little show of stripping down, flashing her ring at him between shed garments. Heat sparked in his eyes with every item that hit the floor, his lips parting, lids drooping. Such a glorious sight, this strong man looking foggy and half helpless from lust.

When she was completely naked, she joined him on the bed. He tugged the towel off and urged Laurel back until she was lying down and he was braced above her. His cock was ready, resting warm and stiff along her belly.

"*Fiancée,*" he whispered.

"Weird, huh?"

"A little. I like it."

"Me too."

"Can I take a rain check on the goring?" he asked. "I don't feel like any fucked-up shit tonight. I just want you and me."

"That sounds lovely."

"Lemme get you ready. Tell me how."

She blushed, from the sweetness of that order as much as her own reply. "Your mouth."

She let her nails graze up his back and shoulders as he edged his way down her body, raked them through his damp hair when he brought his mouth close. Cool fingers parted her sex, warm breath caressing her folds, then his lips. She shut her eyes and searched for his scent behind the aroma of dinner, finding only his soap, not his skin. No matter. In minutes he'd be all around her, his sweat and the smell of his arousal, and the sounds of his excitement ringing in her ears.

Mine, and no one else's, she thought, registering the subtle weight of the ring on her finger. In time the feel and the sight of it would grow as familiar as any other part of her body, and she welcomed that change as well. Like the presence of Flynn beside her as they slept, there was a comfort to be found when something once novel turns mundane. It was the taking-for-granted you had to be wary of. For decades to come, Laurel hoped to slip this ring off and polish it lovingly, feeling dazzled by it all over again, just as this man's rare smile always did to her.

When his mouth had her slick and aching, she tugged at his shoulders, welcomed that sinful weight atop her. He sank deep, slowly, gaze moving between her face and the spot where their bodies met, eyes restless and needy.

"No cramps?" he asked.

"No." A few times in the last couple weeks the IUD had triggered a sharp twinge—unwelcome reminders of the miscarriage—but nothing tonight. "Go as deep as you want."

He did. Still slow, as though savoring each long slide in and out. As though he, like Laurel, was feeling all of this for the first time, somehow.

Before long came those scents she'd searched for, then the sounds of his mounting excitement. Her own rose in tandem, pleasure shifting from a curious hum to a growling hunger. She eyed the cock surging between her thighs, eyed the ring shining where she gripped his shoulder. She reached her other hand between them but he knocked it aside.

"Let me."

She did. She marveled at his strength and physicality in the way he held himself up on one arm, amazed by those deft fingers and by how well he knew her body and what she needed. It was strange to think she'd ever had to teach him a thing about touching her; he could please her as easily as she might herself.

When she came it was his face she sought, locked in those eyes, his name riding the crest of a moan as the spasms swept through her. When she was spent, his hands splayed across the covers beside her ribs and his pumping hips began to pound. "Gimme your nails."

She traced his arms, teasing, then gave what he was after—the mean dig of her fingers in his back as he chased his release. Whether he reveled in the possession of her touch or imagined it as something more akin to resistance, she didn't care. All that mattered was the anguish of his pleasure, the set of his jaw and the power of this body, claiming hers.

He came in no time at all, transformed to a panting, wild-eyed beast, only to go tame and dozy as the pleasure ebbed. He dropped to his forearms and pressed his face to her throat, groans guttering to a happy sigh.

"Good?" she teased.

"Always." He moved to her side and grabbed her a washcloth.

She tidied herself and passed it back. "We've been engaged for all of two hours and it's already Missionary City. You going vanilla on me?"

"Never. Plus missionaries don't eat pussy, do they?"

"If I meet one, I'll ask him."

He tossed the cloth aside and pulled her close, kissing her forehead, filling her up with the scent and sounds and heat of him. His voice was a low and lazy rumble. "If you're worried marriage is going to mellow me, next time I'll fuck you in such disgusting ways you'll be sprinting for the nearest confessional."

"That's so sweet. Thank you, my betrothed."

He pulled back. "Lemme see that ring."

She slipped her hand from where it was pinned between them, showing him.

"It's so shiny."

"I know. I could stare at it for an hour, but I better get busy finishing this dinner."

"It'll keep. Gimme ten more minutes."

"You're the boss."

"In this bed, yes, I am. And I'm not done with you."

"No?"

He urged her to turn so he could pull her close, her back plastered to his front. "Mm."

For a while they lay in silence, rain pelting the shaded windows and the faint tick and whir of the thermostat the only sounds. In time Laurel said, "Things feel right again. Between us."

His only reply was a kiss pressed to the back of her head.

"I worried maybe they'd changed for good."

"They probably have," he said. "Not sure how they couldn't, when two people go through something like that together."

"No, of course. But us, this… It feels the way it should again."

"Amen."

"I hope it always feels this easy. Even after we've been married a decade or three."

"We'll be okay." His deep yawn pressed them tighter together. "We'll both fuck shit up now and then and hurt each other, too."

"I guess that's inevitable."

"But even when we're a hundred there'll still be times when it feels like this."

"When *you're* a hundred and *I'm* ninety-seven," Laurel corrected.

Another "Mm" warmed her scalp through her hair, sleepier than the first.

She ought not to get too comfortable, but she couldn't bear to leave this bed just yet. In a few more minutes, when Flynn predictably passed out. He could nap and she'd dress and finish dinner, and they'd eat and later watch a movie, or maybe just lie here, talking, or not talking, or maybe nothing so innocent as any of those things. Like the shape of their future marriage, like the details of her new career, she'd have to wait to find out.

And until the answers arrived, she'd savor every second of the anticipation.

CHAPTER THIRTEEN

LAUREL MADE HER WAY BACK from the bathroom, edging through a bustling kitchen and out onto a spacious back deck. South Boston was awash in spring sunshine, neither warm nor cool but promising longer days, balmier nights.

It was just past three on a Sunday afternoon, two hours into the party. *Laurel's* party, thrown by Heather to celebrate her new job. She'd been touched at the offer, remembering how she'd envied Kim this attention only a few weeks earlier.

The family had gone all-out in the barbecue department, and when Flynns were told to BYOB, it seems they all arrived with a case, so the beer and wine were flowing like the Charles. The venue was some cousin or other's place in a humble but quiet corner of Southie, strands of Christmas lights and paper lanterns cascading from the second-floor fire escape down to the fence. Folding tables were set up along the perimeter, overflowing with every side dish imaginable. Laurel couldn't help but think this wouldn't make a bad wedding reception.

She and Flynn were seated at the head of a picnic table. He stood, stole Laurel's wine glass and clanked it with a fork to call for silence. "Everybody got a drink handy…? Good."

Laurel took her glass back, feeling her cheeks flush pink, knowing what was coming. They'd kept the engagement a secret these past couple weeks. She found her purse at her feet and hauled it into her lap, rummaging through the inner pocket.

"Toast!" Heather bellowed from the grill.

"Fuckin' right." He held his ginger ale aloft. "A toast to Laurel—officially an engineer, with insurance and business cards and all that awesome grown-up shit."

A collage of clapping and glass-clinking and whoops answered him, and Laurel raised her wine in bashful appreciation, her other hand balled in her lap.

Flynn cast her a meaningful glance and she nodded.

"And a toast to me," he went on, "because despite her brains, I somehow convinced her fool-ass to marry me."

A second's pause, one filled with raised eyebrows and curious murmurs, chased immediately by Heather's, "You what?"

He looked down at Laurel and she stood, passing him the ring. He made a little show of flashing it around at the crowd, then took her hand and slid it onto her finger.

A flurry of surprised exclamations clashed with more clapping, the odd swear from the Flynn camp and incoherent squealing from Anne. Laurel had managed to keep the news a secret from her roommate, much as she'd hated taking the ring off.

"You set a date?" Heather demanded.

They exchanged a look. "Maybe next fall, or the following spring?" Laurel ventured. "I'm not in a rush."

"Little Miss Cautious wants us to live together for a while first," Flynn said.

"Don't put off planning," Heather warned. "If you wanna have it at Holy Cross you—"

"For fuck's sake, come *ooh* and *ahh* at the ring. Let's save the church-wedding-versus-hell-bound-heathens fight for Thanksgiving, okay?"

"I'm just sayin', you gotta book this shit in advance."

"And I'm just reminding you, I'm an atheist and so's Laurel, so don't hold your breath. All right, now everybody get trashed and manhandle my gainfully employed fiancée's sparkly hand, please."

Heather was first in line. "Jesus. Nice work, Mike." As she made her inspection, she asked Laurel, "You gonna be a Flynn?"

"I thought maybe I'd combine them, and be Laurel White Flynn, but your brother said a whiteflynn sounds like some kind of fish, so now I'm leaning toward just taking yours." It wasn't as though Laurel was especially attached to her name, or close with anyone who shared it. In fact, she felt far more endeared to this salty crew than she ever had to her own parents.

"You'd be welcome to it," Heather said. "Class this family up."

Laurel settled in for a good hour's interrogation about all things bridal, disappointing everyone by having zero clue what she wanted her wedding to look like. Flynn excused himself to help man the grill. He reappeared just as Laurel was getting a bit of a break, refilling her glass at the cluttered beverage table.

He wandered over, popping the tab on another ginger ale. "You survived the frenzy."

"I did. Do you think this gets us out of having to endure an engagement party?"

"I'm afraid that may be up to my sister. And she likes occasions."

"The natives were thoroughly perplexed that I didn't have any ideas about dresses or venues or color themes, but they let me live, in the end. I smell brats."

"That you do. Everything's done but the steak." He tapped his can to her glass. "Thanks for making a decent man of me."

"Oh yeah, I'm sure the second I get you down that aisle you'll quit swearing and fighting and find yourself a desk job and a briefcase, Michael Flynn."

He smirked. "Wouldn't hold your breath."

Laurel lowered her voice. "And I would be very, very disappointed to discover that wedded bliss somehow cured you of your depravity."

"Can't be a cure unless there's a disease, and I'd like to think my tastes are part of my appeal."

She tapped his can again. "Hear, hear."

"Only difference'll be that now when you fight back, you can scratch me with your ring."

Something growled low and hot in her belly, and it had nothing to do with hunger. "Is it weird that I just got a little turned on?"

"Nope. Only makes me more certain I found the right woman."

She could feel her cheeks burning but welcomed that heat, letting it wash over her and imagining summer breezes yet to come, the sizzle of champagne on her tongue as they toasted something else in a couple years' time. She didn't care much about dresses or registries, or whether they were married in a church or a park or in the boxing ring in that stinky bar basement, frankly. She only cared who was waiting for her as she crossed the floor. It could only be this man. It could only be those strong hands and those blue eyes, those lips on hers, that body against her own in their bed when the time came to tell their guests goodnight.

"We've got a lot to learn about each other, once that U-Haul's been returned," she said.

He eyed her. "I'm not scared. Are you?"

"No. I don't think I am." They'd been through a hell of a ride together these past two months and held hands through every dip and buck of the rollercoaster. In many ways she'd still felt like a girl for nearly all the time she'd been with him, trapped in a post-college purgatory. She was proud she'd be moving in with him feeling like a woman, at last.

"Lemme see it," Flynn said, nodding down at her hand.

She tilted the ring this way and that, enjoying the slow, smarmy smile that spread across his lips.

"That's a nice fuckin' rock."

"Don't I know it."

"You realize it'll only make me ten times more possessive than I already am."

"That a promise?"

He snaked his arm around her, fisting her belt at her waist. "The worst kind."

"If this wasn't my party I'd say let's pound these drinks and get the heck out of here."

He let her go, shaking his head. "You waited too long and worked too hard for this."

"I suppose I did."

He flicked his finger between the two of them. "This'll keep for a few more hours. Go find yourself a sausage and another drink. Soak up the love."

She looked around, floored all over again to think these dozens of people were here for her. "That sounds like a very good idea."

"I'll still be here, ready to escort your giggly ass home."

"I'll look forward to that." She pulled him down by the collar for a kiss, smelling ginger, feeling the familiar heat of his skin. A humble and happy awe settled over her as he straightened once more, to know this man loved her the way she loved him, and to trust that she deserved it.

With a final stroke of his jaw, she said, "See you in a bit."

"That you will. Go have the fuckin' time of your life, kiddo."

ABOUT THE AUTHOR

SINCE SHE BEGAN WRITING IN 2008, Cara McKenna has published nearly forty romances and erotic novels with a variety of publishers, sometimes under the pen names Meg Maguire and C.M. McKenna. Her stories have been acclaimed for their smart, modern voice and defiance of convention. She was a 2015 RITA Award finalist, a 2014 *RT* Reviewers' Choice Award winner, a 2012 and 2011 *RT* Reviewers' Choice Award nominee, and a 2010 Golden Heart Award finalist. She lives with her husband and son in the Pacific Northwest, though she'll always be a Boston girl at heart.

caramckenna.com
facebook.com/authorcaramckenna
twitter.com/caramckenna

ALSO BY CARA McKENNA

After Hours

Curio and the Curio Vignettes

Hard Time

Her Best Laid Plans

Shivaree: The Complete Series

Skin Game

Strange Love: Remastered Tales

Unbound

THE FLYNN AND LAUREL SERIES

Willing Victim

Brutal Game

THE SINS IN THE CITY SERIES

Crosstown Crush

Downtown Devil

THE DESERT DOGS SERIES

Lay It Down

Give It All

Drive It Deep

Burn It Up